THE
USURPED

Anastasia Shmaryan

Order this book online at www.trafford.com
or email orders@trafford.com

Most Trafford titles are also available at major online book retailers.

Printed in the United States of America.

ISBN: 978-1-4669-3284-5 (sc)
ISBN: 978-1-4669-3283-8 (e)

Trafford rev. 08/02/2012

 www.trafford.com

North America & international
toll-free: 1 888 232 4444 (USA & Canada)
phone: 250 383 6864 ♦ fax: 812 355 4082

PART–I

Have Your Head in the Clouds

Whitmore House

CHAPTER 1

Here remote of an enormous coast in Africa, at the Beach—far-flung between horizons as meets Indian Ocean.

There come into view a couple of dolphins, which are covert at first into deep water. Next, amazingly these Mammals jumped up in the air, and splashing water out fountains on top of their fins. At the rear of the city wide area: coasting via transport making shrill noises.

It's a usual Wednesday mid-day in the African inner City.

The local kids play on a pergola in a park by the beach. A sidewalk vendor sells typical Africa's cuisine, where in corner to the beach—be spectator to a few young people are gladly playing beach volleyball.

Coast line on the beach comes to pass—next is sitting down on that golden dump send a young woman her look come into view being stunning. Color on her hair shows dark brown; and she is the age of mid-twenties. Her name became known—Flora Whitmore to be focused on, as she is stretched her muscles. Taking a big gulp of air freezes to fullest within internal of her lungs, Flora raises her hand up, like gave the impression of reaching for the skies. She feels a minor breeze from the sea—into her flipsides. She stares up, and is glimpsed white feathery clouds, flowing along the air within the blue. The sun excels—resting on the skies, even as a sun giant ray throughout its reflection is plummeting into the wave's stream, where she seen sparkles.

Flora seems is looking meticulously at these dolphins. A beam appears on her face. She then switches her gaze to this young pair, who come to pass, is looking into each others eyes. Next this pair is begun kissing obsessively. Flora's quiet inspiration:—What a nice couple, likely they totally in love?—A sudden changes in her expression—to grim, while she fixed her eyes towards the ocean.

Unexpectedly memories started flooding her, like they began of its thoughts by memory avalanches Flora's mind— reminiscences on her past escapes, which have happened not so long ago . . .

New Haven, Connecticut. The side of University's corner, Flora reads on the door Decal: 'Medical Faculty' prior entering an aim lecture theater. There is enormous audience, seeing in attendance many like Flora's age young groups, who are sitting at benches. She is seated near a young man of an African appearance.

A while after the seminar is over—Flora gets up of her seat; next she headed for the exit.

A young African is following Flora from behind; then he attends to her. As She turns to face this speaker, since Mbeki is making inquiry in brogue English:—Excuse me, do you're going to the next lecture? I see that we both in the same course group, right?—Flora bows her head, and looks at her hand-watch:—I wouldn't know, but we may? Tell, me do you study Medicine too? And if you are in that case us both at the same faculty. But I'm really, in a hurry it won't be nice get late for next tutorial? Don't you agree?—She looks with curiosity to him just as listens. In that case a young man means:— You totally right! And if you wouldn't mind, I can gladly accompany you're after lectures, today, okay?—Flora shakes her head:—All right! Let's hurry up, or we'll be late!—

In lecture hall seen a well-built, intense, clear-eyed, generous appearance is an aged man, with average height, stands in front of group seminar reading to those fifteen scholars—Professor Psychology in Medicine that holds the title of it. Of the conduct a mane with a touch of white and silver grayish on, with common size haircut, of Oxford Don—this is Friedman. He stands in front of a seminar and is reading to those scholars. Between them in favor of the honor he has chosen are Flora and the man of African appearance, whose name becomes public—Mbeki. Scrutiny the scholars Professor Freedman sit off to the side, where meticulously is listening to those, who are gave speeches for their thesis. Next Friedman declares:—Now, between the fifteen scholars, I have selected: Miss Whitmore and Mr. Manringa—step forward with you're presentations!—Then Freedman sits off side, is listening kindly to undergraduates, what they're presentations in order for him, which he does re-evaluate afterward.

At first Flora presents her topic. Following Mbeki, who has also completed his aimed subject presentation, apiece on their ability of opening, which presented themes . . .

A moment after professor turns see to that course group, except each of them profound with their study—unmoved. Next Friedman, takes his reading glasses off, and wipes the lenses deliberately to make the students waiting him. Soon approach the end of lecture—Bell rings.

Later that day on the street in front of University see this young couple leave the build, where they're two strolling outer walls. Flora is near to the man of an African appearance—her co-student, whose name Mbeki - both are walking leisurely, and it the sense of hearing their footsteps down on the surface ground. While this pair is engaged in a lovely tête-à-tête, without paying attention towards others. Flora first is asking:— So, you arrived here studying at University from Africa? Is that right?—Mbeki responds:—That's right! You see in my country it's genuinely impossible to achieve Higher Education or other dreams! In view of that my family had helped me applying in your Nation to study. I traveled in your country to find a better life!—He stops, looks with interest to her, then prolonged:—We talked about many interesting matters, as we haven't got a chance for proper foreword? By the way my name is Mbeki and I have studied in this college for few years. What about you're? How can I call you?—Her respond is with a grin:—My name is Fleur, but you can call me Flora, it's for short! I study Medicine at the same college equally as you're, and I've been here a few years. I wish to become a doctor! You see my goal is to heal people. Since I was a kid, I dreamt too help those, who are sick, treating them well. Back to your question, since we've got acquainted, you asked and yes if this is my birth country.— She stops grins, then prolongs:—In the future with a bit of luck I hope to achieve my goals, and find a job in no time what so ever once finishing University, naturally!—He smiles:—You seem be uncertain, Flora? Don't you worry—you and I haven't finished University yet? Why won't we wait, and see then? We both need to focus on our study that's the most important now, and realism too peak. Later on you and I can wait to see? Don't you think so? In fact, we both need taken the whole lot slowly: Day-by-Day. Cause life is full of surprises!—She shakes her head:—Okay.—He then changes their talk to a new course:—Fleur, are you starving, by a chance? I'm asking, cause it's now pass lunch a long time ago!—He looks at her as Flora in her turn ducks her head—okay. Mbeki proclaims:—Okay, let's go, then?—Mbeki takes Flora's hand—in his.

View next they're both having rapidly crossed the road, and headed for the Café on the opposite side.

Flora alongside Mbeki is walking into "Hungry Jacks" restaurant. There to be seen at least eight to ten among those other customers having seated at the tables. While Mbeki has come within reach of a counter, and attends to one among that staff, who is sighted here; as an employee interrupts talks slowly, but he is using slur words of sarcasm to Mbeki:—What is it feeding time or what?-, He then twists to face Flora—next tackles explicitly her:—And what can I do for you? You must be hungry too? Whoa dew like a burger or Double Whopper?-,

This employee then begins singing, by slowly pronouncing his words:—Always at your service, Ma'am!—Hearing a nonsense she disrupts him, and has grown to be displeased:—Listen you clown, we're very hungry and came here not to watch your concert! God dam it! You're getting paid, and we get served, understood? Don't you dare serve us meal for Rats! Just give us with all that comes on special, dividing for us to be able eating!-

Flora firstly has offered Mbeki a Double Whopper burger. View she has bought for herself a cheeseburger. Mbeki picks up a burger, and in one bite tears down a three quarter of it without paying attention to others, who are in their turn have watched, how Mbeki with gluttony makes that Double Whopper disappears inside his mouth.

CHAPTER 2

A few months have passed. View scenery: skies by a sapphire, where the clouds bordering on fluffy cotton and are floating slowly above the roofs and beyond edifices surface ground, days changing into nights.

In the University's Café is sitting Flora, opposite to her around the table seeing Mbeki. Those two intakes are fried chickens in consumption with drinking water. They both seem are occupied deep in heart-to-heart, whilst its being heard noise and made fuss: deafening say there of resonance of person heard to be exaggerated. She looks in his eyes:—So, Mbeki where are doing after lecture? I was hopping that we can go someplace to have fun? What do you think, Mbeki?—Mbeki replies:—This is a good idea. On the other hand, you know I have not got a car? Unless you are ready driving both of us to that partying?—Flora:—Oh, come on Mbeki! If this is only problem that keeps you indoor? Forget it! I'll drive you and myself to that party. In fact we both are invited! I'll pick you up at seven p.m. sharp! You must be ready on time!—Flora talks enamored:—You know I'm a woman; it's not fair for a man to keep a woman waiting! Right?-

Night on the New Haven's streets, watching two couples are arrived in a silver car with sedan brand. After the ignition is off, those two leaving out the car, while they appeared are wearing lovely clothing for a special occasion. There we view Flora walks alongside Mbeki; entering a house-party, where music played earsplitting sound, in that house seen a large group of young people have been dancing by having a good time. Flora holds Mbeki's hand and soon joined the rest of the group by others, who too are partying here. A sight by those arrivals with air-kissing, have followed by chitchat. Silvia says in a joyful tone:—Hey, Flora good you are made here? And you too, Mbeki!—Flora's voice is with delight:—Thanks Silvia!— Mbeki turns around to watch:—Yeah thanks, Silvia. Where's Troy?—Silvia point hands up and at rear:-Troy's on karate training, he'll be here soon with Jerrod and El. Flora you've missed trainings today? Flora stir look; leans to the left:—Okay! It's always the next time?—She ducks her head, with a smile, and picks up two wineglasses: the first she offers Mbeki. Next she is sipping alcohol herself from a flute. Mbeki winks, takes her hand-in-his:—Flora, would you like to dance?—There a perceived deafening sound of music with those echoes being heard even remote; bracing the house-party enhance—fully with illumination. Inner of that house-party view Mbeki is held Flora in his arms, as they start swirling across in line and around the wooden floor. Those other dancing pairs stop to watch them. When Mbeki and Flora finished dance executions those couples, began gracefully clapping hands. It's fantastic. There various of melody be heard playing aloud, as the young people are dancing as to relax, with their clarity form underfoot steps of echoes under music is on high by full capacity in there of resonances. In company of those, who are enjoining the whole thing with ecstasy, which's emerged to be a great house-party that delayed long past midnight?

Later that night Flora is seated in the interior of a cab next to Mbeki outside has sighted hers car via car-window, which is a silver color sedan. Suddenly hear cell phone is vibrating. Flora's cell phone is buzzing, when she grabs it out of her pocket and answers that call:—Hello! Dad it's you? I was having a party tonight. And I can't return home! Cause us all having a great time here; probably I need to stay at my friends place from Uni. until tomorrow? I'm seen you're and mom in the morning.

Don't worry about me, dad?—A man's voice on the phone:—
Flora, how can you asking me with Mom not worrying for
you? Do you know what time is it? Tell me, where you're now
and I will come and pick you up? Besides, you may have been
drinking alcohol, but you must not drive; besides Flora it's late
hours now. Whereabouts you've left the car then? I hope you're
not driving, are you?—Flora laughs into a cell phone:—Dad
I'm not a child! I know the rules! Cause my car parked near
my friend house. I wouldn't drive now anyway. And so I've
decided to stay overnight at my friends place! Bye, dad! See
you later, alligator!-

At that time Mbeki began asking:—Is the one that's just
called, was your dad?—Flora grins by means of charming look
into Mbeki's eyes:—Yep! It was my dad and mom is worried
about me. Dad was insisting to come here, and pick me up.
I'm nor lying; when's said that tonight I have got really a great
time with you!"—Mbeki beams it's been visible that his white
teethes sparking by contrast to his dark smooth skin of even
with extra whiteness emerge there in his smile:—Me too. So
what are we going to do next? I see you aren't in a hurry
backing home . . .—In that case he began slowly is brushing her
lips, following with kissing. Next those two advanced, and are
addicted into deeper kissing.

The night, at dormitory's room is seen Mbeki slowly flick

Flora's lips, and boom—their dance lasting, while both are leisurely getting undressed. Flora and Mbeki pour are into kissing, their hands move fast resting on each-other skin coat. They're looking hungry and desperate for love, and slowly sliding into the bed . . .

To view through a window the moon shines up there that has a gift for this pair with its ray's reflection.

The next morning Flora stands next to Mbeki in the medical laboratory, sees among them in attendance are within Laboratory that large group of students—dressed on white robes, as all the doctors typically do.

There is also present Professor Friedman.

Flora on the scene is whispering close by Mbeki lure into his ear; while her lips moving on his skin:—Thanks for a superb night. I was thinking about you the whole time. I couldn't even concentrate on studies. Next Friedman gloomily points a finger at Flora:—Hey, you're in the group! Get sorted your private matters outside!—Friedman is leaning his head towards Mbeki, who says gently. His eyes with a stare, and he points towards fellows close to him:—Me too. Shush, we'll talk later.-

Its late afternoon in Mbeki's room at dormitory, where he is lying in bed beside Flora, and both passionately kissing each-others lips. Flora's face so close to his ears, as whispers into, while he's being able to taste her lips in that facial part, Mbeki's closeness with sensation of his manhood that gave her pleasure, seeing as her finical grin eyes-to-eyes are close. Flora:—Do you want me to stay with you tonight? What about our exams? Cause if you do wish, I'll make you very joie de vivre. In fact we both will be practicing to make love— feeling in high spirit tonight! Don't you agree, Mbeki?— Mbeki murmurs into her ear:—Please, stay with me. I want you . . .—He, then half opens his mouth—with a passionate kissing, which follows.

It's a usual Saturday afternoon. The sun is not bright, seeing as its late autumn, cloudy. In the city center comes into view Flora walks beside Mbeki. This pair stops is begun kissing, where people stroll in that area by looked peculiarly at this couple. Flora and Mbeki are into a flavor by their emotions . . .

Twilight coming behind from the city—sees is this pair walking towards cinema.

At entrance hall appearing Flora and Mbeki, who are just come in cinema's vestibule. After they have paid for the movie tickets—next are walking in. As they are stepping into the theater, where the screen panel has appeared, and occupied antechamber.

During the screening this match up has created its own self-reliance during that film session, given that they covered under dark drawn by close sits, and they began kissing, just as whispering into each-others ears, all the time in theater. Flora by enchant whisper:—I feel so good, darling and mine only wish for that tick slowly be fixed on. While a visitor breaks into and says in a grim tone:—Shush you! Don't disrupt us watching the movie!—The pair looks at each-other smiled; cover oral cavities. Mbeki whispers into Flora's ear:—Bar, ah! It's great to know that you feel satisfied, so is I Fleur. Will you stay with me tonight?—Flora is voice altered with regret:—I can't, darling, not today. I'm afraid my kinks may be mad, and can make a big deal me sleeping outside my home. I'm getting set in lieu of their shame?—Next Mbeki lightly brushing her lips. Her act is being in reaction with lasting kissing.

Here the Whitmore sitting in the family room, where are hearing their echoes. There have come into sight a group of people that strikes to be Flora's father—Karl; her mother—Virginia. There are too seen an aged couple one of them, who is Flora's grandma—Mrs. Kathryn; at lasts but not least grandpa—Hamish Whitmore being the same age as his wife. There has also appeared a teenager in his eighteen, who is Flora's brother—Jason. Else they are all having got engaged in a frown argument. Sees the living room enters Flora, who resound being heard through her footsteps; and she is wearing on a pair of shoes in high heals. Given that she is busy to take off the coat, as her dad Karl, deals with his daughter, and he is uneasy:—Flora, can you tell us here, where you've been?— She reacts:—Dad you ask me the weirdest question! I was in University, naturally!—But Karl is displeased:—Then another fad. Why you were coming home so late night? Even a few times you haven't slept at home? Tell us?—Flora is annoyed, and talks by scorn:—Dad, you know that I'm an adult, and over eighteen? I'm very busy now with assignments!—Virginia talks calmly:— Flora, dear, your father and I older than you, actually we are adults here. And we feel like to meet your new Boyfriend? Why won't you bring him to meet us all?—The Whitmore's glances to one another—they are looking stunned.

It's sundown. Flora is sitting in her room, around the desk, has bowed over the computer, writing. Next she looks be confused, and walked out rapidly.

Out in Jason's room hear a knock at the door. He gets off his bed, and nimbly is walking to open it. By fasten the doorknob he sees Flora, who comes out with a pleading face, and a nervy smile:—Jason, I have problems with my project. Can you hook me up to Internet, please?—Jason:—Sis can't you see. I'm busy? Give me some time. Let me finish my new game "Tomb Raider!"—Views Jason is deep in the play station, full of activity into his game. A short time after by completing it, Jason switched television into the normal TV programs, where out of the blue on the TV screen appears be heard music shown "Mama Africa" song televised. When he tries to switch channel, it seems she absorbs a device, by using mean words in a heated tone:—What the hell you're doing? Leave that channel! I want to watch and hear this song! Once the song is over and anew picture comes into view on TV, Flora has pressed remote control. Switching attention towards her brother, Flora curiously engaged in:—Jason, do you know what's song called?—Jason's head leaned; he is curious:—Sis, I do not know. Let me check a preceding channel?—She then asks:—What was that song titled?—Jason:—It was on TV called "Mama Africa"! Why you want to know? It's not my type of music, cause I prefer Rap!- Flora is thrilled her eyes spark:— I love it cause it's artistic! Did you see the nature was shown there fab? Can you tape for me next time?—

CHAPTER 3

At least two weeks go by. At dusk Flora is speeding on South side of the main road. Next her car remains still through the traffic jam. Her eyes is hard, concentrating directly with the cars racing over by trying overturn her, while the visually is blurry from a remained mist outside up there in the air. But she stuck in a traffic jam, as difficult, as it seems Flora had interchanged to find a way to move forward.

Meantime, Flora makes a call over her cell phone. Mbeki is sitting in Dormitory room deep in his thoughts. As the phone rings, he answers the call, parallel, lazily gets up moves with languor, and answers in a deep voice into phone:—Hello! Flora is it you?"—While Flora has stuck in traffic, looks in car-window is blurry, but she is imagining: there's no-one there expect for Mbeki and her. Once Flora returns to reality, she dials a number, and talks on her cell in a charming voice:—Hi darling!

How you're doing?—He's voice on the phone:—Where are you now Flora?—She on the line is responding:—I'm in my car, returning from my normative Marshal Art training. It's such a bad luck! I stuck in Traffic jam. But don't worry; I'll be home in no time what so ever and wait for your arrival at my place. Mbeki you didn't forget my home address? Did you?—Mbeki responds:—No. I have written correct in my notebook. Flora does it really matters to you? As you think it's a good idea for me to come up to gather with your family? If you think that's polite? I see you later, Flora!-

At this same night Mbeki arrives in time in a cab and stops near Flora's house. The moment Flora glance Mbeki through window; she is hot on her heels runs to meet him. While Mbeki paced, crossing the front lawn; there he has spotted her. Flora and Mbeki are hugging. Next the pair together is crossed Flora's front doorstep.

When Flora alongside Mbeki is appearing in family room, where a group has turned up. One amid them is an aged man in his mid-life or early fifties; tall, fair-haired man with mixture of gray amongst; blue eyed, and dressed conservatively on. Here is a lady shown up, being in her late-forties, longhair, with dark brunet round a bushy within her head mane, as too fully clad on nicely. There is also seen—a teenager, being in his eighteens-years of age, alike to he's father's look, with curly hair, estimated tall. There comes into view an old man in his late-seventies and elder woman alike in the same age group of her early-seventies, by seeing there elderly couple, whose hair full of silver gray nuance, by full bushy within both those women onto their hair—she is nicely dressed. Seeing the strangers Mbeki smiles; and strides toward them with greeting that he shake hands as etiquette allows, between with those are in attendance.

A while after the introduction the entire group has been seated around table, as well opposite from each other. Soon the feast started. Still mostly all the Whitmore's observed the new comer. But the atmosphere between their connection, as well adjacent has felt tense during the whole course of meal there for the rest of that evening and beyond. Then Karl is broken silence, he smirks is tackling cynically:—And so, you're arrived here from Africa, lad?-, Mbeki says be proud in brogue English:—Yes, that's exact, Mister Whitmore. I was born and bread in Africa!—Karl's curio:—How and where you two have met? Do you're too studying Medicine?—Hearing the last question Mbeki beams, when is declared:—We've met in University! Cause both are studying at the same Faculty. Likewise Flora, I want to get High Education and become

Lawyer!-, Karl talks with sarcasm:—It's interesting to hear! But have you made plans for the future young man? What are you going to do, when you accomplish your studies in this country?-, Mbeki reacts:—You're daughter and I've been in the relationship quite a while. And I would like to take the opportunity asking for your consent to marry your daughter?—Karl then turns facing Flora; he appears pale of a shock with eyes wide-open; addresses the young man is edgy:—If you want my opinion, you both neither have completed you're not studies, nor achieved Degrees from University, yet?—Karl prolongs:—So, your mom and I think that two of you rushing things with such important decision as Marriage. Don't you agree Virginia?—Then he spins around to face the whole family in the room:—What the rest of our family thinks about? What's you're view of this odd Mrs. Kathryn? How's your view sir on it? And you're, Jason? Hey, you all!—His wife, takes over of talking, even if Virginia is by a nervous grin, but speaking in a tender voice:—I utterly agree with your father, Flora! There's nor hurry in such important matter as marriage!—She then takes breaths, looks dull; and continual:—Besides, what place you two going to live in? Karl and I worked all our lives! And we won't be able to help you two financially. Most of this entire grand house belongs to you're Grandma and grandpa! Likewise we've your younger brother, who will finish High School soon. We'll be seeking for his prospect to study. It seems we unable accept you're two under our roof!—Karl turns to face Kathryn:—Am I wrong here Mrs. Kathryn?—Her palms open:—No you right. If you two are ready to get married look for a place to live? Perhaps, you may young man return Back to your native soil?—She then stops. Next she attends to Flora:—Why'd you be making plans for the future as to marry him Flora?—He stops sorts out with Mbeki to bring about:—Mbeki, did you apply to be granted permanent residency in our state, yet, or you didn't?—Mbeki looks lost; and hides his head in shoulders:—Not yet, madam. I'll do it soon?-

Mbeki strides throughout the whole room towards Flora's relatives are sitting in the room. Karl turns around:-Goodbye, young man and luck! Tonight . . .—Next Karl turns towards the door. Mbeki is saying goodbyes to the entire Whitmore family:—Thank you, sir and too every one in your family!—Next Mbeki walks in the direction of exit. Then again Karl returns to look at TV, and is watching programs, when held a book in his hands. While he follows with a stare to Mbeki headed for the door; at last Karl glued his eyes into TV screen. Mbeki exits. Acting the rest of Whitmore's isn't following Mbeki to the hallway, as to single his steps out.

Out in the walkway appears only Flora, and holds Mbeki's hand in hers, whilst she's walking alongside him. Sees their shoulders feel each-others auras of a magical deem. By enter into the hallway. Before leaving Mbeki is facing Flora, and both are glanced into each other's eyes. Next stepping over the porch this pair is embraced, following into a passionate kissing.

In time, after Mbeki's exit mood amid Whitmore's seems being like a cat on a hot tin roof. Barring Flora breaks the torture silent, by implying in annoying tone, loud:—Mom, dad, what's wrong with all of you're? Why you spoke to Mbeki in such mean way in an attempt to offend him?—Karl barges in:—I don't think, Flora that you in the position now to condemn us? It's one point. Secondly: we did not ask you to bring here someone that happens to be more than your friend?—Karl inhales, and is continuing:—At last, but not least, we won't accept him as a member of our family to be! Basically, who's likely to be your future husband?—Now Flora stops him, alleged in hot temper:—You're wrong dad and you too mom! Because I do love Mbeki, and want to marry him, if he will ask me too!—Virginia is in a calm voice:—Flora dear, you're father and I, with everyone in this family wishing for you the best in life! Aside from our disliking Mbeki, we as well trust our judgment!—Virginia looks around the room for support; by taking a deep breath. She then ongoing with her discourses:—This young man, Mbeki isn't the best choice for you! Those former men you have got involved in, when you're dating your ex-boyfriends . . . ?—She stops, then takes deep lungful of air: Virginia, who is unbroken by a way revealing of her state of mind:—As for Mbeki's African heritage: we're all jointly objecting for you picking him, a black man to be in a relationship with? Perhaps you may consider having his babies?—Next Flora's Grandfather Hamish, in line gets a word:— What I'm concerned about hereafter, carefully thinking: in a point of good judgment. Still our personal views offend you Flora? Cause of my delicate analysis about Mbeki, and beyond your affair? I'm just reflecting on situation, which's obvious—he is using you, my dear to remain in our country, and taken advantage of you in order to gain permanent residency!—Next Jason talks fast:—That is quite what I was going too say. I don't give a dam if he is black or not. I agree with grandpa. I think it demit obvious that Mbeki is seeking the way to stay here sis, and too gain residence in our country?—Flora in a rough tone that enlightens them in temper:—You wrong! All of you're, and you too Jason! Mbeki is a good man and the whole thing as you've just said about him bullshit! I'll do what is in my best interest and pleasures! And If you are against our relationship that's your problem? As for me, I'll carry on meet with Mbeki! If you're continuing resist our liaison? I can move out of this house to a dormitory room, and live there with him?-

Karl is upset, and in pleading tone:—Don't go Flora, please! We want what's best for you. Believe us you're making a big mistake, Flora! You'll have a great career ahead of you? Flora, you our daughter and we love you! As you'll regret to single out that so as to get involved with Mbeki?-, But Flora stops her, is heated:—I don't care what is going to happen next? I'm happy now! Dad and mom, please accept our relationship, as it is? I Love him, and he's make me feel full of ecstasy!—Hamish, tells be crossly:—Watch your mouth young lady!—She is pleading:— Don't you all wish for my happiness?—Karl's of qualms:—We do! I'm sorry, my poor child. Sadly for me to say, we can't act on that. Do it either, as you were told for our! Unless, you on your own in that affair?—Then Virginia interrupts him, and advices:—Let me talk sense in her? I am sorry; my poor child! Hopeless we can't do that . . .—, Karl has also interrupted, when begun protesting:—No, I shall tell her! Flora, you either do it, you've told our or you on your own in this affair! It's your choice and we are not joking! But if you disobey me?-, Karl stops, then in a despotic voice:—After this day, Flora forget about our family!—Flora looks to all be sad; then tells:—Well, dad if that's how you all put you're demands? In that case, I am moving out of this house!—

Later at night, sees Mbeki is in dormitory's room—makes a phone call to Flora, talking into the phone:—Flora, how are you doing? You sound sad, what's going on there?—Flora's voice sad on the phone:—Mbeki, I am so glad hearing your voice!—He talks into the phone:—Do you have problems with your family, is that it? Cause of me? Flora's voice on the phone:—I can't talk about over the phone. Will you mind if I move in your Dormitory room?

At dawn—as Flora's stuff whole has been packed.

Soon she is started taking luggage downstairs, out in the hallway, without the family became aware of her decision, and before they're all awakens; besides she doesn't like facing them. Unexpectedly her dad Karl strides toward hallway, where he has caught exact Flora's movements. As Karl sees signs of—he comes within reach of Flora; even as his aim to shield the doorway by using of his broaden full-body complexion. Flora is in contrast—determined to leave, sees her head being leaning down. Karl instead challenges her implying even if he looks tense, says loud:—Flora, what're doing so early up? And in the morning with all my stuff?—Flora takes a deep breath by self-reliance, the same as she declares, as bobs her head down, but she talks delicately:—Yesterday after we discussed I thought of your terms, dad! And so I've made my mind to move out of this house. I am not kid anymore! Can't you see to I'm sure want I to make my own decisions in life! It does include my relationship with Mbeki or anyone I hope to have affairs!—Sudden is hearing are footsteps—together Flora's mother Virginia alongside her son Jason, who is following at the back, walking into the hallway. Virginia has been dressed in a nightgown; and there is sighted Jason—in pajamas. Jason is rubbing his eyes; probably he just has awakened. As Virginia's expression changed to a dramatic paleness, and the trio has glanced on each other been bewildered, as they were lost for words. A while has passed. Flora's dad breaks the silent; a turn he tackles his wife. Karl appears is of fret with a finger pointing to the front door:—Can't you see Virginia? Our daughter dogged to move out of the house, what do you think about that? Hah!—Virginia is distressed too cry:—Flora, my child is that true? Why? What have we done wrong to deserve that?—Flora looks be distressed and in heated voice:—I'm not a child anymore! I want too make my own choice embrace and be with a man, who means a great deal to me, and not as you're disliked! Yesterday you offended the man that I really like very much. What's more, all of you're against my relationship with

Mbeki? And that is unacceptable to me!—A moment or two one and all become silent—are looking at each other, as their shoulders trembling. At last Karl breaks silent, even if he is alarmed, talks in a deep voice, declaring:—Well Flora, if that's what you want? Then, go ahead, leave! But I'm giving you last warning either come to your senses or stay home, or leave but don't get in touch with all of us . . . ,—Flora takes deep breath; then is grabbing her stuff, and walks out via the doorway outer walls.

Later saw Flora enter dormitory room, and is carrying a luggage along with her extra stuff. Then without delay she gets settled in—is checking a regular size closet. She began pack entire empty shelf with her stuff. Later she is searching out the drawer, and placing her stuff in Mbeki's regular size closet. Eventually Flora finished with unpacking. She then affectionately has raised an issue to Mbeki:—I see your bed isn't adequate to rest on and yet it didn't bother me before, why should it now, right?—A stop, as her eyes spark with glow, when she implies:—I'm sure the two of us likely to live in comfy?

Don't you agree, darling?—He is lost:—Ohm, yeah. Ohm.

CHAPTER 4

At least ten days have passed. In the campus Sport Complex is emerged group of young people, between who comes into view—Flora. Many of them are sitting in the leisure room, which shares the space in the Campus Bar also is a part of the Sport Complex. On the chaise langue there are come into sight a group of students all around that space some of them sitting with a stare into TV screen. Troy Vitale, Silvia Ramirez and Eliot known as El; sees Flora is between them too. Troy—a young man in his yearly or mid-twenties, very tall and slim, the ex-High School Champion of the athletics, knowingly in high jump sport. And he is with fair-haired, of light skin tone. Next to him are sitting Eliot and Jerrod. Troy is medium-to-tall of height; his mane color brunette. Jerrod dark fair-haired and is alike earlier guy medium-to-tall of he's height. He's skins tone a bit tan; he is at the same age as those last two

Troy and Flora. Just then Troy is drawn near Flora, while hear resonance and within that spacious place, and begun flirting with her, and being boyishly charming:—Hi, gorgeous! I'm sure you missed the last trainings? Cause I've not seen you for a jiff. Where were you? Were unwell, Flora?—She is shaken her head shyly:—No me was busy with coursework!—Troy looks at her, talks with charm:—No shit? I was worried about you!— Flora reacts:—You shouldn't! Listen, Troy I didn't see you at that house-party?—Troy is lost:—Being busy. Flora, tell me do you seen anyone at present? Cause I'm aware you broke up with Jeffrey Witter a while ago?—Flora looks as is stunned; her eyes wide-open:—Who told you that? Bah, Sil-vi-a?—Troy turns; he is concerned:—Look, Fleur it's not my business, but from what I heard your ex-boyfriend still has feelings for you? Jeffrey it's his name?—Flora's waver her head. In that case Troy continual with discussion:—So, Jeffrey probably does what he is basically can to win you back, Fleur?—Flora seems is uncaring:—Now, my goal is to become a doctor and to heal people, as well love kids. Once I graduate—I wish for a job involved kids. Apart from that I want to have kids of my own!—Troy has a boyish look, and with charm in a sweet talks:—You're kidding? I love kids too! And can't wait too have mine! No don't be timid I am just teasing you!-

Opposite from them are—Silvia, Jerrod and Eliot seated. Seen as one of them get up of sits, and have come across to hear their chat—are looked unhappy. Then those three are having turned their heads—to watch TV screen.

At the same time in complex arrives a man—medium height but muscular; he emerged be physical strong and a capable man; with a nice short-haircut, who retains a Black Belt in Karate. His name's Kyle, he seems be in late thirties or older. He turns out to be the coach pro groups of Karate and self-defense. Kyle comes within reach of Flora and Troy, as signals to the rest of this group too come close, ands says in a deep voice:—Hello, boys! Are you ready for today's trainings?—The whole group in unison is proclaiming:—Yes, Coach!—Next this coach turns to face Flora, and tackles her alone by a frown look:—What about you, young Lady? You've missed few lessons. Were you sick?—Kyle turns is facing Flora, seeing her being confused; but she responds—deceitful:—No coach! I was busy with my coursework!—She then bows her head down. People of that group, in contrast shake their heads and made a sign—thumbs down. Troy beams, say with a deep intonation, but is ironic:— Come on, Flora, we know these assignments! I like you're too have good times. Here's a query: who is this lucky bustard?— Then Kyle has interrupted Troy, implies towards entire group, and in a commanding voice:—All right group! That's enough! Flora, if one more absent from the course group and you'll be out for good! Are we understood each other? The same goes for all of you?—Flora bows her head down; Kyle is rejoicing then implies again—dominantly:—Come on guys! We have lots of exercises to do today. Don't waste my time, and let's move it!—

Out in sport complex—group entering sport roomy within University. Ahead is walking Troy beside him sees Eliot and Jerrod are at the back rear; evenly following those Flora with Silvia Ramirez. Sees those lasses at the rear Troy stops and holds the door wide-opening for the girls. Silvia's eyebrows are puckered up, next Troy implies:—What? Don't you like me being polite, Silvia?—Silvia beams, with approval:—All right, Troy! I hope you're boys won't change in ten years time? If you'll only be for the best!—Then Eliot joins the chit-chat:—You have sounded like dirty Ramirez! Pro Russian-Scottish population?—Flora and the rest of that group is begun laughing. Silvia looks be displeased:—What the Hell? Your talk's Bullshit!—Silvia left and she along with Flora lurching for a seat on the bench—aside; at once they have begun watch those pairs, who wrestled in the midst of the spacious premises.

Meantime, Kyle approached those three and let them know: when their turn will be. After Kyle has left between that group of young people begin a differ kind of discussions Troy is leading speaker:—Dudes, raise your hands if you have ever wrestled a Midget or in medical terms Dwarfism?—Jarrod and Eliot have begun laughing, put palms over their mouths, but Eliot have slowly deviously raised hand up is excited:—On my try, I haven't! But I wish I have done it!—Amid those dudes are begun extreme laughter. Then Jerrod still is amused, entails:—El, how do you think they'd feel? Since you're tall, akin to stick of figure? You wouldn't like too take on Dwarfs? Ohm, or little people, as they're preferred to be called such? Eliot is supporting:—Don't you worry about me! I'll give the Dwarfs or little people a fine striptease! They'll call me—'Destiny's Child'! How about that? Ah? The rest of that group among guys burst into hysteric. Shortly while Troy talks as laughs:-Ha—Ha—Ha! El it's bullshit! Dudes we haven't been choosy, trying to sleep with any nature of lasses, without the chic, who aren't venereal carriers? Dudes you're not with me in that?—Jerrod is cynical too laughs:—You're right, bro! I think we practically are capable medicals. Given our profession involves are doing proper check-ups for all chic! Ha-Ha!—Eliot means:—I am with you and for that! And if need to be an expert in obstetrician the only way for me is to practice often. And it can suit to be a superior Doctor?—That group in chorus:-T-r-u-e!—Next Troy alone adds more:—True! Even if I is not trying, but I'm fairly positive that for every Pot there's Lid! And for every Man is a Brass Ring! That's all we can afford now?—Jerrod smile, in quirk of fate:—Some of guys go for that type of wedding plans slip in flowers. Did you know in the world are over thirty five weird breeds of flowers to get ordered with extra stuff. Can you imagine flowers? There's a flower identified by as Dusty Miller!—Eliot looks be surprised by it:—Nor shit? Bah? That's why you called Silvia Dirty Ramirez? You're bastard, you know Jerrod?—All silent. Next Troy said is serious:—That's bullshit, bro! Speaking of flowers, look at Flora?-, Troy knits his brow is up and points towards Flora:—I assume that she hopes for diamond?—The young men are jointly:—Ha-Ha-Ha! Why not look on other girls? Troy is pushy:— They're like an exhibition! Women by their nature like more to exaggerate than it has really are. Women talk too much it's typical for them! For my part yet I'm down, cause I prefer to fuck a gorgeous girl! Then think for outcomes later.—He's head leaning to Flora, and brows up, by a grin. Jerrod barges in:—Troy you're not wary with chic instead all's casual?—Troy responds with confidence:—Yeah, but in its place. Now I'm attracted to Flora! And don't you dudes warn me, at time? I'm in that mood for pleasures! I pick Flora!—Eliot looks at him, quivers back and forth:—By the way, Flora now is dating Mbeki. Aren't you unaware of that?—Troy's look has dramatically changed to gloomy:—No, shit? Dam it . . . !—Suddenly Kyle by line of attack on those is enlightened:—Dudes, don't you have enough disputes? Let get to practice. Move it! Get in pairs to wrestle!—There also sees bystanders and a few pairs are executing in the course of having put self-defense style into practice—central to the room.

CHAPTER 5

Another two weeks have passed. On day session view in lecture hall Flora is writing in note pad, and seated at the side of Mbeki, who's doing, just as she—deeply has concentrated in writing on student's subjects. Hear there are echoes, which of this preceding Friedman is lecturing undergraduates. Given that he has demanded of the medical course group to be set for a question paper that each of them being pre-occupied of overwrought with their focus. There's that group of scholars—each profound within their exams—unmoved. Among those see in audience at the heart of tutorial—Mbeki, who sits at the side of Flora's bench is facing a test questioner. Aside of that group, at the heart of tutorial is sitting Friedman observantly waiting for undergraduates to stop. See next Friedman takes his reading glasses off—wipes the lenses deliberately of silent to order the students:—Hurry up—with ample you're assessments!—

Soon after comes the end of that tutorial; and so is examination—bell rings.

After that bell is heard, Friedman turns to face that

Tutorial and makes reads monotone:—Listen every one; you've got lots of time to complete your thesis. Now you're time is out!-

See Troy completed first his written test—then other of those three of he's friends, have followed. Mbeki has too done question paper on that aimed subject. See Flora there hands over her assessment at lengthy time—separately, but be the last one?—

Anon Mbeki walked out in hallway following him in back is Flora, who spoke to him; saw he seems being troubled by something?

Suddenly a group of guys come forward to this pair amid them are seeing Troy, Jerrod and Eliot. When Troy tackles

Mbeki; and is leaning his head towards Flora says be cynical:—So, boys and girls! We have heard that two of you're going out? Is it true, Mbeki?—Mbeki who pulls his brow up:— That's right Troy. Flora's my girlfriend! Just for one more inner topic:—I'm looking for a day job too squeeze into studies! I'm short of cash, men?—Troy takes a pause; he then began talking of scorn:—Why not hook up on night shifts to lift heavy sacks or bouncer in the Night Club? Flora has links there? Don't you?—He winks. Flora interrupts him, and interferes in men yak, means:—Troy, Mbeki is absolutely fab. He's witty, erudite. He deserves decent jobs! We both need that!—Troy is out of wit:—Okay! Slow down, Flora! You have to know this Guy, what? Let say a few months?—He is raising his hand, and points a finger at Mbeki, Troy implicates:—Hey you're, Mbeki! What's you're feelings to Flora?—Mbeki smirks; winks to her in accent:—What about Flora? She is a clever girl, and a great friend. We are just the right couple!—Troy is sarcastic:—Really? You haven't met Flora's Ex-boyfriend, Jeffrey than?—He looks at Mbeki's reaction; by apt shakes his head. Troy says more:—I thought so; you've got a lot of mystery? Anyway lots of us are mates here, except you, Mbeki—not live across the street from us? Cause you an alien in our country!—Hearing Troy so-called him, the group of dudes are begun smiling. Flora shakes her head, and comes back with a retort, looking of joy, as is talking positively in biting wit:—You're all have a great sense of humor? So, Troy getting a bit competitive? Are we, boys?—Troy is cynical:—We certainly are? But we know how too put in practice! Aren't we dudes?—He glances at this group of, while apiece have given their bobs. She is heated; her cheeks turn pink:—Aren't you a smart ass? Why not bite your tongue Troy?—Troy next turns towards Mbeki means, and by insulting tone, while expressing slowly of lexis:—Mbeki, you arrived here not long ago from nowhere? And already taken the best crop of the course! So you've hooked on Flora then?—She too replies with bad humor:—Troy! That's not of your bloody business, which I am dating? Besides, I'm not a Crop and you're surely nor the combine harvest! Troy you're all forgetting—I choose on my own. And mind your own business?—See all are footing, while they having emerged ogle—heated caught unawares. From nowhere at the back is advanced Freidman, who gets involve, when interferes amid these groups, which already seem being sulk. Friedman lilt in bad humor inquiries toward that group:—Excuse, me gents, is you're gathering okay?—These groups emerged pretended are calm. Next an act in respond, by which Troy has composed; but he's voice is out of wit:—Professor, it's nice of you to be concern about us. We're adult, because dispute between us is out of your typical area. Given that talk's of a private affair. True?—By a twist he then refers to the rest of the group; they act of bob with his heads in response as be on agreed. Friedman's alleged:—This is paradox, Mister Vitale, if you think that I'm unaware of life events? In that case you're wrong!—All awkwardly shut up. Troy is witty:—Absolutely not, Professor! I wouldn't dare? But we have our theory . . .—, He is getting interrupted by Friedman, who still talks is witty, but in sharp lilt:—You a smart ass, Mr. Vitale?—Next Friedman circles is pointing finger to both Flora and Mbeki; next is attending to them:—As for you Mister Manringa, and you Miss Whitmore I need you're two follow me? We have a topic to discuss. Gentlemen—my apology. Let's go in my office then, you're two . . . ?—

Professor is entering into auditorium style class; following behind Flora and Mbeki are holding hands-in-hands. Yet Friedman comes on the edge of table; sits at surface. He then pulls head up in that way he does by eyebrows; Friedman addresses those two at once:—You know young smart nation, I was working as a psychologist for many years, so look by Logic. I had got to meet pairs, what's come to light eminent obstacle between them is trust!—Mbeki gets involve:—Professor you know I must admit am astonished, but you're right!—He is pushy:—Besides, if the pairs find that trust, their love could complete both of them with pleasures!—Flora's eyes glowing as she say with delight:—Professor it seems, you hit into exact aim! We have found love and trust, is not it, Mbeki?— Mbeki has become distracted:—What did you say? Yea, that's right!—Friedman glances into Mbeki's eyes, shakes he's head; he then swaps to Flora, meaning:—Well, juveniles, now let's talk about you're tasks, separately, shall we? Do you mind Mister Manringa, if I discuss first with Flora?—He's civil, but of fret:—Not at all, Professor. Bye!—Friedman politely:—Goodbye, Mister Manringa, and see you're later!-

After Mbeki's disappeared off room; Friedman next turns, as his head leans aside—facing Flora, while him being likely to discuss on:—Miss Whitmore, I'm curious, how long you two have been dating? It seems to me you have bonded a short time ago? Am I right?—Flora is at a complete loss; talks calmly:— No Professor, we're dating almost three months. I even left home to live with Mbeki in dorm. Still, it's hard fiscal times for us. Knowing for Mbeki and me tough won't be forever? What is your view, Professor?-, Friedman's head leaning, he is wary:—Who knows? How long hard times can seize? Most important is what will lies ahead for you both? Flora, do you love him?—Flora:—Of, course! I would do anything to be happy with Mbeki! Why are you asking me, Professor?—Friedman talks passionate:—But does he love you? Cause love is a powerful thing! At times it can blind you up, as we befall to it, on the way loosing our merger. But if one isn't wary throwing yours into that emotion; at some stage can end up—either in paradise! Or be brought down on your knees and one ends up in hell!—A Silent—He's term grown to have affected Flora; thus she looks shy; reacts is nervy:—Professor I don't follow you?— He then advocates:—Miss Whitmore, before I'll try to explain my practice as a Psychologist on meaning of love, you must be absolute certain if your partner being honest? Cause at time your life can be put on the line! It's really crucial that any of us retain! Yet, can we get back to rework all the result of your test. Flora at my faculty; it's the key to success? — She is confused:— Ooh, yes definitely, Professor!—He means:—So Miss Whitmore what I'm concern here is that you're insufficiency to study gone down? I don't mean to imply that it's the cause of your Love? But I also aware that you've got talent to become a Doctor in the future. And prior you've enhanced it. I follow your progress a few years; and it's critical for your success, given that it is a short time left to graduate? Now, I'm not so sure that you're keen, Flora?—Flora is fretful; so her panting:—You wrong, Professor! My want to become a Doctor! But my happiness is important too me to. Now, if you pardon me, Professor, but I'm off? Have to run!—Friedman then takes his reading glasses off and wipes the lenses deliberately—of breaking silence. Friedman then puts back his glasses on using one hand pull up his head; that he proclaims be calm:—Miss Whitmore, I hope you've got a hint of my counseling?-

As Flora walks towards the door, prior exiting—acts in response as is skeptical, but her head bent forward:—Yeah, Professor, I neither can, by nor means!-

CHAPTER 6

A few months pass. Tight on the New Haven's street. Outer surface is snowing, near to dormitory. Though its day, but up in the sky appears—overcast. See in the room Mbeki, who's reaching for gifts that Flora in the past few minutes has handed over to him? As he says be joyful:—Hey, Flora thanks very much for the gifts! I've never had one of this before!—She bemused:—Oh, gifts to you for the upcoming Christmas! Hey, but Mbeki you're joking about gifts?—Mbeki says in a deep rough voice:—No, I'm not! In Africa we genuinely are poor and existing without getting extravagant gifts. Don't look at me like that, it's a fact!—Flora utters is taken aback:—You're kidding? Is that true?—

A while pass. This pair still in Mbeki's room, which is your basic room from hell in dormitory. At that juncture display: posters up on the wall, with incredible clutter of junks;

bookshelf full to have themes of literature; magazines and others varies of stuff. Traditional jewelry made of ivory or elephant bones and to gain other goods—outward shows of typical African customary souvenirs is arranged there sighted, which part of he's African time-honored myths. There view in best position extra to that stuff on display: cheap jewels, a mirror base cosmetics dangle-up are on that surfaced wall; with main things, which having owned by Flora.

View—Mbeki and Flora are kissing. After a while being alone their intimacy has grown, as Mbeki and Flora are feeling attraction that is cherished into involving them. In unison as Mbeki kisses her on the cheek, by means of Flora is addicted, and submits to passionate kissing that grows—into love making . . .

Later he kisses her on the cheek, by which she submits too as is ardent into a passionate kissing Mbeki . . .

CHAPTER 7

One day as Mbeki is in dormitory's room—reading a book. Next he listens to: two knocks at the door. Next he with laziness gets up his seat and a walk to door twists that knob. When Mbeki twists that knob, door gets open. On the front doorstep turn up are two of kind strangers. When they saw Mbeki, one of those visitors by a strict eye is dealing with him:—Excuse me, please; we' are looking for Mr. Manringa?—Mbeki is confused; reacts in a deep voice:—It's me. How can I help you?—

Meantime, out in the kitchen Flora is preparing lunch in the commune kitchen. There sees a middle aged woman has approached Flora, who turns out be dormitory's manager. By draw near Flora; she then starts inquiring her with a grim look:—Flora, dear you and Mbeki haven't paid me for this month rent. When are you planning to pay?—Flora's face altered, as she looks edgy:—Mrs. Rosh you know that Mbeki can't find a proper job? On top of troubles we're busy practices for final exams! But I swear that when we get the money I'll personally pay you. Rosh shakes her head; grins:—Flora, dear, you're both can call me Laura. I know you're two busy by swing engagement such as sex?-, Hearing that Flora freezes, a yak follows. Flora looks confused; with a shy pitches this:—Mr. Rosh, I don't follow your question?—Rosh bobs her head:— Flora, I'm all set, are you two set? How often you make love? Or having sex? Just answer me intuitively?-, Flora with a stare at Rosh still she is freeze; act in response:—Okay, I'm all lost Mrs. Rosh? I can't figure out, what it has to do with you're learning me?—Rosh with a concern look:—Its lots to do for both of your future! Causes I must evaluate why you're two talented students now turn how to put more exact? Practically be the worst Scholars? But don't forget I was a counselor long ago?— Flora is sarcastic:—Obviously satisfied! Often for around the clock, and if we're not studying with no breaks for the whole thing by camasutra. Even with no eaten; non-stop for the entire night. How's break?—Rosh smirks:—Flora that's impressive! But remember, love can put you on TOP of the world, or can destroy you wholly! You're can forget what is reality; and for you two the focus on now?-, Flora has a wicked twinkle in her eyes face turn into pink nuance upon her skin surface that being compare to a naughty child, as this lass is answered back: Flora tells shyly, but looks is confused:—Mrs. Rosh please don't embarrass me like that. Mbeki and I now in a hard fiscal situation. We'll pay you for the room, I promise Laura!—Rosh has a sly smile:-When it does going to be Flora, dear? Bah . . .—, Flora seems be tensed, but sure:—Give us some time, Mrs. Rosh, will you?—Rosh changed be serious:—OK. I'll wait. Now let's change the subject. You've got some visitors arriving at your place asked for Mbeki-, Flora disrupts looks is puzzled:- Are you sure, Mrs. Rosh? You know who they're?—Rosh bobs her head:—Yea I have only heard that they were asking for Mbeki. Those two then have entered in . . .

Back in Mbeki's room the second visitor looks odd at him, and declares:—Colleague and I working for immigration. Are you Mr. Manringa aware that your visa is expiring next week?—Mbeki's face turned to pale:—If truth be told I didn't think about that. I was hoping that since I'm studying at this country in college. I'd be getting . . .—, Mbeki's interrupted by one of the two visitors, who's sarcastic:—Ooh, I see. Have you at least considered come up to our office? To discuss about your future plan with our dep., Mr. Manringa?—At that time in the door appears Flora and looks with wide-open eyes, her look be fretful inquires to Mbeki:—Mbeki, what's going on here? Who are the people?—Mbeki is nervy in a deep tone:—The people are from immigration department!—Then the second visitor turns to look at her:-Hello, there! I am Joe Manson. And may I ask who are you? What're you doing in Mr. Manringa room?— She looks worriedly:—My name is Flora. I'm Mister Manringa girlfriend. We are getting married soon!—Those visitors have exchanged with eyes look. Then a first visitor—made eyes contact:—It may not change his disposition.-, He turns—points to Mbeki:—Agreed by Mister Manringa, you must come on a scheduled time to see our authorities.-, He tackles Flora; on his face catch glimpse of beam:—You can come along if you wish, Miss Whitmore?—Flora reacts with courage:—Ooh believe me, I'm going to do that.

CHAPTER 8

Saw movement of clouds in the skies. Outer surface—with a massive snow fall. View Flora's holding Mbeki's hand as approaching a bulky door upon it outer surface is mahogany nuance that tinted with linseed color. Sees this pair up on the door decal: the Judge Honorable R. Gibson. Before enter that office Flora and Mbeki look at each other; by taking deep breath; they're having knocked at the door.

A recruit among the law enforcement widely opened a heavy door for this couple, as has invited to come through in.

This Judge Gibson looks via he's glasses, as reads; next he his tilts head up and nonce addresses both in monotony voice:—So young people you have decided to get married? Is that correct?—Prior to answer Flora's cheeks turn pink, as says clearly:—Yes, you're Honor!—Mbeki repeats like her:—Yes, you're Honor!—The Judge:—Have you young woman got a consent from you're family? As from what I can see—there isn't anyone from Whitmore's members, present here, at such important occasion or I'm wrong?—Flora is tense:—Yes, you're Honor! I'm an adult, and had got out of maturity trialed age; as you can see. So my decision is to build simply own my future. Isn't true, Sir?—The Judge is skeptical:-You're right getting married be the most important day in anyone's life. And present of your parents are fundamental! As well the two witnesses from both sides is also significant!—Flora has got heated:—Unhappily, but in my case it is impossible. My family had refused except my relationship with . . .—, Signs to Mbeki. She then is unending tells story of their love . . .

In that case she declares to the Judge:- . . . And for that reason Mbeki and I've decided to get married without my family's present at the wedding Ceremony. So, you're Honor, please let's get done with the procedures, and . . .

Night out of the mist a car has driven on surface of the ground is covered with snow. It stops near club. That happens to be Flora's silver shiny color car-model of a sedan. Within the car seen has seated apart from Flora and Mbeki another younger couple. As ignition has got off those four leave car, where Flora and Mbeki appearance in focal point of the group amazes: sees her hair and dress that designed for a special event outfit that compliment with their proud postures, as they're looking stunning. Those four leave the car, where Flora hair and dress be designed for a special, and Mbeki's appearance elegant, for both wore in fashion—superb, as the pair proud postures and their looks are stylish. As Flora and Mbeki view other couples—amazes: their hair and dressed in occasion with proud postures—are looking stunning.

When those four stop nearby club's entranceway with exuberance of echo being heard from inner, in combination with deafening played music. As the sliding doors opens for those four, once they enter the Club just at that time Flora and Mbeki holding their hand and are passing by bouncers. In the interior of the club come into view shimmering of desired illuminations, which are flashed around the whole area. There is heard music with sound on a full capacity, seen those folks are radiant overflowing with enjoyment for forthcoming—New Year celebration therein. One among those four—leads the way ahead of Flora and Mbeki, follow half-a-arm length behind, and he is walking in the lobby. Set of two pairs pass through these huge crowds, besides those uptowns appearing in club, mostly of who are wedded couples, or in affairs.

Suddenly some women acquaintances are greeting Flora with hugging and air-kissing; yet some of them have an awkward look towards her companion, who holds her hand. Flora has not paid attention; still she is glowing, given that she married Mbeki after all. On this unique night two of them are not only come here to rejoice New Year festivity, bar Mbeki and hers celebrate their marriage ritual. In a view of that Flora laughs alongside with her husband Mbeki—a supreme wedded couple.

Just before entering a reception area hall another young couple has called upon Flora she turns around, and began smiling on the spot as has approached by a new young pair. Flora with a wide smiles, and proudly points at Mbeki:—Hi, Betty and you too Frank!—As she turns to face Mbeki; takes his hand declaring to them:—I want you to meet my husband, Mbeki!—Betty looks to Frank both with atypical look:—Hey, Flora! Welcome to the Club!—Betty and Frank stop, have glance at Mbeki and begun turn their attention to him, but Betty alone stated:—Excuse me, what's your name? Fleur you said?—Mbeki reacts:—How due you do? It's a pleasure meet you too!—He tries shaking hands with Betty, who offers half hands fingers to him. Betty and Frank's eyebrows turn up with atypical look at Mbeki, as he talks to him with dislike. Now Betty says, but Frank is silent:—Hey, how you've been? If you wouldn't mind, sir but we would like to talk with Flora tête-à-tête?—She then turns back to Flora.

After Mbeki withdraws Betty starts speaking up her mind to Flora with a stern look:—Flora, what your family has though about that marriage of yours?—She stares at her, says firmly:—From what I see you similar to my family, who have objected too? You also want criticize?—Then Frank smirks, be poise:—I personally have nothing against this guy, Mbeki I believe?—Flora duck her head:—That's your life, Fleur and you can live to see, how it's going too turn out?-, Just now Betty has interrupted they're gossip, and alike has expressed her opinion by dislike:—Look, Flora, we're respecting your decision. Even so if it's rather goes wrong? You always can file for divorcé. My brother, Jeffrey is a Lawyer! He can help, if you need it?—She alters being heated:—Betty, we have just only got married, but you're already talking about divorce? Can't you both be happy for me, once? I love Mbeki!—Betty and Frank have begun shaken their head. Flora starts rushing:—Have to run, guys! Happy New Year to all of you!—Betty is diplomatic:—You know, Flora, my brother always was more than caring for you is . . . ,—Betty stops abruptly, as bites her tongue; and smiles:— Ciao, Flora! Happy New Year, and good luck!-

All around in the club laughing are appearing joyful.

She is searching for Mbeki—passing through that massive crowd of public. Flora spins to view Christmas tree that being decked.

When Flora at last is found Mbeki those two get into a passionate kissing.

At dawn Flora wakes up in a hotel-room, near to her in a honeymoon bed ensemble stretches out—Mbeki. Now he is her husband. At that point in time—Mbeki is asleep.

Flora meantime, starts recall what has happened on day before . . . Flora surges in her mind to recall: neither her family had shown up at their wedding ceremony. Nor they have called to congratulate both of them or spoken at least to her, from the time, when she was absent. Flora thinks:—Despite all obstacles I am feeling happy. It's the beginning of a new life for me and Mbeki: as Husband and Wife!—She thinks. There is catching view—a bottle of Champagne with two wine-glasses be situated close at hand on the bedside-table. Finally Mbeki rouse and climbs on top of her, in tight close is hugging, brushing her lips are moved into her neck; and shift lower with more kissing, follows. Mbeki is stretching his arms to get into relaxing and a comfy pose—stopping at the way. In time, whilst Mbeki to fold over both his hands he is brushing Champagne bottle via his upper limbs. Flora sees that bottle falls down and hits into the ground through light-yellowish nuance sparks from the sun's reflection passing through mirror image of liquid, as it falls into surface and spills around. She speaks kindly:-Hmm!—Mbeki shifts closer to Flora—eye-to-eye:—Don't worry about Champagne! I was right picking you among others, just then at University corridor. She by charming murmur:—Whoa! Oh, dear husband, believe me I'm the lucky one! I'm feeling on top of the world. Because last night was, with over satisfying—alright . . .

It's crack of dawn. See in immigration office this same man Joe, who is sitting in his bureau—round the table. In the office visible chairs, computer with equipments, which are required in such establishment? Next to be heard someone is knocking at the door, Joe with laziness gets up his seat and walks to open it. A view of doorknob voices being heard behind wall. When this Joe opens the door on entrée are having appeared Mbeki and Flora, who are held hand-in-hand. Seen together—they're stepping into the office. Joe smiles, his hand extends to shake with Mbeki:—Good morning, Mr. Manringa! Nice to see you're. You came just on time? I see you've brought along your girlfriend?—Flora joins the banter is uneasy, but proud:—Good morning, Mr. Manson! I'm Mrs. Manringa, if you don't mind is my name now? He and I've got married a few days ago!—Joe smirks watches the intruders:—Well congrats to both of you're!—Mbeki is edgy, as his eyes wide-open:—What news have you got for me?—He turns to face Flora, Joe looks at her, and takes a deep breath. Joe bends his head down, and began reading papers, as he is ongoing dealing with Mbeki:—Mr. Manringa I am afraid, your student visa is expired. Even if you were married citizens of this country, you have to give us reasons for your claim to be successful. Firstly do you have a stable income to support yourself and wife?—Mbeki shakes his limbs, in a deep voice:—I'm still was unable to find stable job. I still need some time before I'll receive my Bars as a Lawyer.— See Joe's upper limbs are trembling:—Secondly, have you got assets, which you own or want to pay for?—Mbeki's lost, said awkwardly:—My wife and I are looking for a place to live, and in time we both will be . . .—, Joe twists, whilst is address now Flora:—What about you're young lady? Do yeah own assets, property? Or ready sponsor your Husband? Or any of your family members can become pledge for your husband's future to secure Mr. Manringa funds?—Flora bows head down of regret:—Sadly for us, but they can't. My family likely neither accept our relationship, nor to be our sponsors! They'd declined our marriage, even refused to help us fiscally!—Joe looks in their eyes one-by-one:—Nothing I can do for both of you're.

Sorry to say, but in compliance with the state Law you're Mister Manringa—illegal migrant in this country, who visa is expired! Be decided: you must depart, without delay. In case if you refuse, you're to deported or put in jail.—

CHAPTER 9

At least two weeks have past. At midday a shiny silver sedan stops near to the street of Flora's house. Mbeki too is siting in the car as ready to drive off. Seated in the car Mbeki bows his head down:—Flora, I need to drive in a place?—Flora turns her gaze close to the car-window. She looks in his eyes:—Mbeki will you picking me up?—Mbeki clings to wheel, as switched on the ignition. He's by half-whisper:—No. You catch a cab. I'll meet you at home! Don't be too late, Okay? Our flight is to be in a few hours?—Flora is with a nervy smile; shaken head, as her limbs shift:—I know that. OK! See you, darling!—

Flora slowly opens the door, and steps out off a car. She then steps in Whitmore's corridor, where glanced grandma, Kathryn. She is striding inner, in family's living room. Suddenly Karl, her dad, shows up, looks dazed; seeing his head, is leaning to the right. Her mother, Virginia—in contrast is fulsome; without ado she is begun screaming. She is joyful, blaring:—Son, come down, quickly! Flora is returned Home! Jason! Where are you, Son? Hurry up!—The Whitmore's staring at Flora, who's breathless:—Mom, dad, I want to be in you're company, here and now?—Virginia delicately:—My girl, of course! We are your family, despite the whole mess! Fleur, you're for ever will be our child!-, she looks in Flora's eyes; then has continued:—Flora, why you look so serious?—Next Mrs. Kathryn, who first is leading Jason for room; sees behind is walking lad, both are heading to. Sees young Jason comes down into family room. Next in the row is Grandma, Kathryn pursued with a length behind. Jason is excited to talk:—Sis, are you come back home for good? I hope?—Flora talks slowly but is edgy:—No! The reason for my coming is that, I need to talk to all of you!—Flora takes a deep breath; explaining:—If you know, I'm about to finish my study in med school?—She stops; composes herself, continual:—As immigration did not let Mbeki to stay? And not gave him green light . . .—, She is taken gulp of air; and rolling:—And so, we have decided return back to Mbeki's native Africa!—Virginia is expressing her grief, by way more like of is mad. Next to her is Mrs. Kathryn is crying; as they all are following Flora with their eyes; as she climbs the stairs, until vanished in corridor that leads upstairs. Kathryn seems be disturbed, when sank into a comfy chair; fold over hand on her upper body, like is set for a prayer. Equally has her husband, Hamish on opposite side. After hearing such kind of news the Whitmore is from heed about Flora. Mrs Kathryn like a drama queen:—What you think of Flora's fate?—Karl's eyes wide-open:—She gave me a shock!—Hamish hands fold on his upper body:—News shocked me and Kathryn as well!

Meantime, at New Haven city street sights Troy Vitale by himself is coming out from a Café. Next as he attempts to cross the road . . . When from the corner is driving fast a silver 'Sedan'—at the front. Impulsively the auto stops sharply; and blocks Troy on speed, that looks alarmed; then steps aside being in shock. An eccentric has driven in a 'Sedan' almost knocks Troy out at a close range. One before long gets out of the car. A person appears is Mbeki strolling at the road directly to Troy stands, which's rolled over the front car-window; seeing he's being falling down on the ground. Troy is gnashing his teeth:—What the fu** you're doing? Mbeki! Are you crazy? You're almost have rolled me over with your fu***** car?— Mbeki bobs his head; puts his right hand into pocket. Still he leans as looks with a weird ogle at Troy. Mbeki nods his head talks quietly:—Hey Troy, too you to! I did not see you coming on me?—Mbeki with an odd smirk that seem rather creepy. Troy is edgy:—Cut that crap! You know demit well, how to drive!—Troy turns soften, as is smirks in a cool saying:—Listen, Mbeki, how it's hang in?—He else winks of irony at Mbeki, whose facial expression suddenly changes to grim:—I mean with Flora? You're two still seeing each-other? Or all gone and forgotten?— Mbeki's hand pulls his hand out from pocket, where he hold small alike a gadget or so that, Troy is spotting it. He leans to Troy, and is half-whispering into Troy's ear:—Listen, boy! And listen well!—Mbeki stops; then is talking with biting wit intense:—I saw you're friends . . .—, He points a finger straight at Troy:- . . . being with Fleur? I know demit well that you try too rising up into her?-, Mbeki has got interrupted by Troy, who is gnashing his teeth:—Shut the f**** up! I'm not your Boy, demit you!—Now Mbeki cuts short Troy's utter, be edgy:—A boy is how we call like you're, in Africa! Differ between you and me that, I'm in her pants now! Do you know why? Cause I'm a Man and you are a Boy!-, the last words have made effect on Troy; as he ready to start a brawl. Mbeki's leaned his head, and signs with eye-brows down on his pocket, where a small object be hidden. Troy's look is changed to gloomy; as he still talks cool, but edgy. Mbeki talks in command voice:—That's right Boy! Now a word of warning for you: forget about my wife, Fleur!—Troy alters as turns pale, with wide-open eyes at Mbeki. Mbeki responds as if he is edgy:—That's right! Fleur belongs to me! Say goodbye to her! Cause she travels with me to Africa!—Mbeki then turns his back on Troy, and strolls towards his car. Sees Troy is left looking with a shock to Mbeki, who drives off on high-speed.

Pro tem in Flora's house she climbs the stairs, and steps into her bedroom. Now, she departs—leaving behind her bedroom. She was attached to this room. Now she takes a last look round a place that for many years was like a fortress for her that has given her strength and comfort here. Flash back: Flora is reminiscence of her childhood . . . Next she lies on top of bed-covers. Game—'Tomb Raider' that brother, Jason gave her as a gift once ago; now it's become dusty. Staying in her upstairs room, Flora has taken the last look round her bedroom. Flora's voice sad too cry:—For years I have collected that stuff. The room was my fortress, like once it'd be helping me maturing . . .

On a whim hanged mirrors fall down there; sees shatters into fragments. Flora has broadminded by logic; is sadly whispering:—This sign is for bad luck? It couldn't be happening to us now? Not when Mbeki and I are united? I would rather forget about the whole thing . . .—

Then Flora slowly is closing the door behind with tears pouring down her face . . .

In family room—she freezes, close between doors; looks at her entire family—more than ever towards her dad. While her hand hold on to a medium size figure flipside—is an amiable Virginia, Flora's mom, with tears in her eyes rolling down her round cheeks. Flora is crying, as moving to exit:—It's time for me to go!—The Whitmore's uproar:—Flora, we Love you!— Except Echoes, this is heard, and have faded away into the air . . .

Flora takes a look the one last time; and is kept on deep breathing. Seeing as the cab is driven her away quicker . . .

PART—II

In Africa On Venture

Acacia Tree & Gazelle at Sunset

CHAPTER 10

Flora and Mbeki are arriving in Africa in the morning not to be a flight of the minds eyes. Still at the airport Flora follows Mbeki in back.

A bit later on half-way of the road—genuine traveling on picks up autos, of which they're having waited a long time to catch one. Mbeki bends down, talks quietly:—Cabs here are out of service run!-

After a long wait see a truck stops; s the driver be in favor of cash. The driver says in poor English:—You've to pay me in $US Dollars only! I want only cash in hand!-

Still on typical road Mbeki soon is letting her know of their next form of transport that they must switch to horses wagon. Mbeki:—Our next form is going on horse's wagon! If we're lucky to catch one, naturally?—Flora looks be lost and dazed:—What are you saying? You must be kidding?—Then she grasps to be true:—It's actually called Horse and Cart! But how can it be?—Finally, out of sand dust a single car is rushed near; passing through Flora and Mbeki; with an exception of non-stopping. By a long remain Flora rest beside Mbeki sees from a gap, slowly is galloping cart with a donkey—moving towards them. Mbeki:—Now I see a horse-and-cart come up towards us, down that long road . . .

Entering Manringa housing that is like a hut; Flora has sensed inhere bad smell; of haze within the air. But she wouldn't dare make queries or complain off that . . .

Inner of Mbeki's family hut comes into view at least four

Africans, between which are having emerged an old woman in the age of late seventies. This black woman seems is staring into Flora strength of mind; alike she has begun feeling goose bumps upon her skin texture . . .

Flora befalls by the old woman's spell, and invites Mbeki with her eyes wide-open; gently:—Mbeki explain it's odd, why is this old lady seem staring at me? How . . .—, Instead he prevents her from saying is fuming abruption; whispers in her ear, by angry shout:—Shut up! You only speak, when I tell you so!—

At nightfall Flora goes with Mbeki and this old woman into the open-air in their family's front patch. Mbeki points her to go behind:—Follow me and grandma out.—

Mbeki is also pointing a hand at this old black lady; and lets Flora know secret, which's kept her in suspense.

Mbeki grins, and is saying with pride:—You see this old lady, is my grandma. Her name's Candela! She was destined to be a Witch-doctor, back then in her youth . . .—, He stops; takes breaths. Flora, in contrast looks is amazed. View Flora's eyes wide-open of curiosity:—Is she really?—From now, he affirms her be clear:—Yes, Candela was! And she still is a witch-doctor in our community!—Apart from being dressed in colorful dress the African woman has shown off upon her head-wrap, positioned is covering over her head. On the patch inspiring but weird is happening, which was facilitated in advance by this old African woman—Candela Manringa.

There sees Flora is beside Mbeki—having seated down in company with the capable African woman, grandma Candela.

Then Mbeki tells more:—My grandma knows a lot! It seems she could see through one's sole? Like she saw through yours tots up . . .—Flora sits alongside Mbeki, who holds a hen close toward flame, which has burned. View the old African lady is rubbing these stones that have made of ivory; as being availing through her palms. Acting, as it appears Candela is shuffling them around sand—with those bones. A circle has been prepared; Candela then produces from tiny old buckskin a bag with quantity of elephant bones. Next this lady has thrown fast those ivory stones down into the ground. Flora whispers into his ears:—Honey, what Candela is doing here?—He bends down, and gave her an idea about stones:—Do you see ivory is glossy on sand?—Candela is studying flashes for a bit, just make out what's future to be?—She starts waving to dash by switching back and forth in front of Flora's eyes are chanting delicately; that this last one's being slowly converted into timid. So Flora gets spellbound by Candela; that sees lulls; as her eyes are grown heavy, and lids droop. Like hypnotic Flora is gliding down; then lies down on the sand. Flora is in illusion her mind overflowing of memory:—When she hears Virginia's low and tender voice:—Roses are red, violets—blue everyone's asleep, and Flora should too . . .

Quite a few weeks have past since Flora's arrival in Africa. She lives with Mbeki in he's family housing hut. As mood between the Manringa and Flora seems is intense.

During that time Flora has tried to find the way to be helpful to other family members. She doesn't understand the language; along with an African way of life there.

On one occasion Mbeki tips Flora to go work in family's patch. Draws near, by using a superior drawl as to deal with her, Mbeki spells out his ruling, with domination in a firm voice:—Flora, you should wear a shoal! Now it seems that you and I are not longer in the city? You see, in our rituals the women obliged to cover themselves from top to toes.—Flora looks be bewildered:—If that what's wanted of me to do?—

CHAPTER 11

All but fortnight bypasses. Flora has worked plot of land by now is missing her family and friends liked often to bring up learned of memory. She is working in a place similar to backyard; given her being slightly negligible through that extend plot of land . . .

Out of dust appears a jeep is driving straight into the patch; this has resulted on shocking these home-birds away. A jeep stops by a short gap of width, where Flora is doing labor on. Those new arrivals are leaving the car; given that one among them without hesitation starts addressing Flora in French. The first guest says a deep voice in French:—It's urgent, where is Mbeki?—

When Flora turns round, is shy and points a hand to the shed talks in French:—He is inside the house.—Those guests are begun walking away; passing through—directly towards the Manringa hut.

As Flora enters the house, sees here a few guests are having conversation in the company of Mbeki. He instead does not pay attention towards Flora's being there.

. . . Mbeki emerges being quite intense; into debates with those. Flora couldn't understand a word of they're troubles. Except for one cliché that she's overheard; as those guests stated.

A second guest talks in Swahili tongue that she doesn't know:—Give us in Tanzanian shillings?—(This is the Tanzanian State conventional currency.)

In that case Flora sudden has intruded between the gents; her interest into their discussions, being excited she is imposed, in French:—Excuse me, if you wish to hear me out? I speak French! Gentlemen, can you tell me, if is a school round? Cause I live here and I'd really like to learn your language . . .—, one among those guests smirks. Mbeki turns to face those, which between them likewise gives a sneer. The guests are seemingly opposed; when emerged just having looked daring and defiant. When Mbeki splits up a belt off his trousers, then a sudden smack, he's unleashing over Flora's upper limbs, is hitting her chest. It is caused her falling down on the ground. Mbeki repeatedly smacks! Strikes Flora again; seeing as he's thrown punches over her other body-parts. Through his upshots it has made Flora froze and still down. Mbeki still is in point of striking; seeing him looking angry; he is also shouting in French:—Ferme ta gueule!—Given Mbeki is started with uproar that him being jumpy, as he began talking in English:—Get the Hell out of the room!—View Flora is in a state of shock staring, as her hands held up in the air attempting to shield herself against Mbeki's lashings, seeing as bitter tears have rolled down Flora's cheeks.

By a force Flora's unclasp fell open designate be seen on its own; lying on the floor. Sees Flora's shoal slips out that has covered her hair, on the whole of those two weeks inhere . . . It's be a warning sign for Flora to back off; so she slowly started crawling away; is unaware of Mbeki's atypical deed. Those guests are given a smirk, while having absorbed Flora, yet they're having a chat with no paying attention to her with him under pressure.

In front yard Flora is watched from distance those guests are leaving hut; and walking beside Mbeki, who's staying a full hand length away from them.

As those guests are entering their jeep that has been parked on the brink of Mbeki's shed. Follow of those jeep drives off; but Flora is staring as their car vanished.

Eventually Mbeki turns sideways that, close to Flora's stand; only then glance at her. Still Mbeki watches her with practical and captivated eye. Her head moves up and down; while she stays put, being by unsaid opts. Flora's wisdom thoughts:—I found him odd? How he behaves? It's just strange?—Flora is unaware of Mbeki's reaction; she still boldly breaks the silent with a concern look, as exclaims:—Mbeki you've changed since our arrival here. Why? What's the matter? Are you in some kind of trouble? Talk to me!—Mbeki yet again is deep in thoughts; then without rushing, looks her in the eyes. As it seems he's being troubled by something. Mbeki then is declared him being edgily:—My family has awful money problems! Cause we were indebted to someone. I hope the whole thing can resolve to be secured . . .—, Mbeki gains himself yet again; sees he is being annoyed and raring to go; and loud in English is one of a two-faced, he protesting:—And don't ask more questions . . . Go! Work around the house! As you go and clean up outer! Then in the lawn, and do it faster!-

In the morning, after malnutrition lunch in the family kitchen, Flora has brought up an issue to her husband of that previous incident. Sees she is upset to cry:—I've been insulted by you! I need a reason for that? Mbeki, talk to me!—She is solemn, but hysterical. And Flora is expressing her stance to

Mbeki being heated, but gently:—It's disgusting the way you had behaved on day before. You were attacking me in front of guests! Why, Mbeki?—He composes; and in contrast acts in response, while turning his head away from her towards aside, he's by annoying lilt:—It's for your punishment! You have disrespected our rituals and the way of life? Do you understand? Also I must remind that you is living under my family roof!—On sunset be seated in room Flora recalls past incident, when Mbeki's bashing her . . . So Flora has assumed calmly; cause being critic of, her mute decision:—I won't make a big deal out of our earlier clash, as if it let to slip that? I wouldn't be able to defend myself if dare to defy their ruling, cause its all clear to me. Honeymoon is over! And so it is!—

Live in her husband home has affected Flora, she would carry out all dirty work around the house; on a plot of land as an extra. Mulling over, she cleans pooh done by animals, on top of an old lumber-room out-of-doors the ward were built toilet. So Flora mumbles to herself:—I have to rake for hay and grass . . .—, she inhales:—I want to be in my home's turf?—Flora began remembering her family home and the lawn there . . . Flora is back to reality:—Soil here is dry through its core down advance? This is not quite as to be unusable? Or is it? Well . . .—

CHAPTER 12

Meanwhile, another few weeks goes by in Flora's new home that she has made—in Africa.

One night Flora is seated in front yard—discussed about Mbeki's family dealings; as if he has appeared in unusual light, from the time when arrived—he become a changed man. Mbeki then puts to her plain and simple; as being heated, and pushy:— My family and I insist that you should go working on the field, side-by-side with other neighborhood? What's more, Fleur? Before your return home on the way, you bring for the whole family two buckets up full of clean drinking water. This is what I accepting!— Flora reacts by inquest, aloud and is looking uneasy:—Why you're doing this to me? I have never worked on the field before. Else I don't speak your innate language? How in the world I'd be able understand what locals say? For all intent and purposes in my connection with your local Africans?—Mbeki in his turn says be irritated:—I don't care! Tomorrow dawn, you must go on the field! That's out of question! Is that understood? Cause if you Fleur ignore my rules, I warn—you will be punished!-

Then one night, by entrance to Manringa shed, while Flora is getting ready go to bed . . .

When Flora enters her and Mbeki's shared bedroom she saw a blanket covered with cushion that's lying on bottom of the ground. While Mbeki makes clear to her, points his hands down towards. Mbeki in a harsh voice yelling:—You won't be sleeping in this bed! Go over there! I've placed a stretcher bed there! Cause from tonight on, you obliged to sleep in corridor! Go! Move away!—

Later going to sleep Flora is undo stretcher-bed so as to make comfy. Lights off—instead are candles flaming within. Flora lies down on top of the rags. At first her eyes open; murmurs to herself:—I'm feeling so ashamed . . .—, Saw as tears are pouring down Flora face. She then closed the eyes:— Still, I can't sleep?—She is weeping, being uneasy, by an effect Flora pulls back towards other side. Follows that she shrinks away—into previous position.

View it's barely morning light on; Flora's already up; slips on clothes with extended skirt, which has exposed only her bare ankles; and atop a shoal that covered her head from tip to toe. She shifts in the open air to a set place for washing herself up; then is sensed underfoot a turf ground. Flora has briefly washed her face; just then brushed her hair.

Firstly Flora picks up two buckets; with no eaten snack; she exits for the field be unaware, where to go, or what site to?-

. . . Given one tool left in toolbox that, she be supposed to utensil for; and working with a blade. By employing a blade is to cut off crops, sugar plant, by which Flora inexperienced in sort of labor.

Her condition worsens; by motivation become most serious; and she is being unable to understand African dialect.

On the field—in temp job Flora is given to carry out a task of hard-hitting; she's following the rest of these groups, which are working. Scarce goes, as Flora achieves that aim somehow, is progressed by slashing crops, of employing a blade.

In her effort to make into each stroke . . . Seen next as she is being moving ahead . . . Flora murmurs by heavy pants:—I'm feeling so exhausted—working on the field. Jesus, I can imagine how those Africans feel? When it gets toughen? She goes up stand; breathe in; to rest a bit; guessing.

Later on she draws attention to:—How long before break comes?—Given that she has not been used to tough labor; with long working hours in the fields; through her thinking . . .

. . . Still its being a painful blister emerged upon the skin texture of Flora's hand.

So, she shows to one, who's giving orders pointing on her hands, that being harmful of the skin.

By day's end with last of her routine jobs on the field, Flora takes off. Then she suddenly:—Oh, demit! I recall bringing two buckets with clean water in Mbeki's house?-

So far Flora is feeling down, and disorientated to be in middle-of-the-road. She tries to find aimed location with tap water. Flora politely in English asks one there:—Can you point to the road? To clean water taps, please?—

. . . Lacking of making contact with those Africans puts Flora in distraction; given that those are kept ignoring her.

Later that night sees as she has arrived Mbeki's shed empty handed; is footing at porch without water. Mbeki's started yelling by abusive cliché. Mbeki signs by hands; be angry:—I blame you for defying my orders!—Flora is confused timidly:—This is not my fault. I didn't find water taps or a tank!—But Mbeki interrupts her on top of his lungs; calls her being heated:—Flora, you're a lazy, white whore! Why didn't you look for the Well?-

Some weeks pass: Flora kept working on the field; and has located the well on her way . . . Sees her hand is covered with blisters; and face adjusts to tan; also is spotting upon her skin nasty sunburn. Still Flora is unable to say a few words to Africans; yet locals are ignoring her company if she attempts word for. Even if she is working, just as tough, as the rest of that African public on the field; and under high temperatures . . .

From this day on Flora repeats visibly, as it would develop into desperation for her, as is she trying to fit in, on the field:—Fitting among them, and were getting adopted to African life-style undeniable, is impossible! This is without ending for me bad luck . . .—, She is panting; as talks to herself, and thinks:—Genuinely the natives' way of life being tough. I want understand the language? So far it has made me feel like an emotional retard?—

No less than a week pass. End of the day is approached. Flora figures out that her job on the field at least is over and done with, for this day. Also a man in charge there gave her the low down, that he says-so in brogue English:—Your job for today is done! Put down your blade. And leave the meadow now, go home, Mrs. Manringa.—Flora is glad, and murmured to herself:—Thank goodness, for that . . .

And happy Flora does abandon the field without stop.

Africa—Acacia Tree

PART–III

Trade On Flat Terrain

CHAPTER 13

Upon Flora's arrival home in Mbeki's hut, she is glad to get a rest after a long and tiring day. Still, it hasn't been that simple. In its place Mbeki is ordered her, and is insisting, while he talks in a superior voice:—Me and my family are going out! And you too have to go with us! You Flora, follow me and my family to a flat terrain . . .

As the family left shed, Flora has followed them, even if they walked on foot for quite a long time in a weird far distance, where Flora observed the regional that, seems be identical to the Northern African Savannah.

In time see Mbeki with his grandma, Candela are walking ahead; following in back other members of the Manringa. Given Flora is walking being the last in line that loyally goes behind. Still all the Manringa is walking for a long time far a field, towards secluded area.

Next it comes into view that crowd amid locals on flat terrain are uproar ahead; as of right be heard; which having surrounded by chorus and drumming. Its click to Flora as is sighted that panorama of a barren area; next view of gathering to be held here . . .

This captivated her eye as she has found a way round.

That Mbeki made explaining to do; she is excited, but most curios. Flora leans towards him; as signs her hand:—What kind of event is offered there?—He says proudly:—There goes on a ceremony! Among our folks from the Tribes that is called Mijikenda!—Flora is curio rapt; as gently asks:—Did you say Tribes? And what loyally they're . . . ?—Flora stops; is looking at Mbeki's family; as cools, calm and collected. And she made queries; as is curio, in a flash is amazed:—I meant they're rejoicing? Where do all those folks come from?-

Here comes into view are these leading crowds that well thought-out having prearranged event pro those Africans, where have set in it wide area. It seems ritual is held visible, which has drawn in all those neighboring from African districts. General publics in attendance have formed a circle; where they're singing approximate a few yards from Flora's standing. Besides those folks appear are dancing established of African tribe rites. There're women performing uproar by earsplitting, using their tongues through noisy flicking, which resounds of common echoes. All in chorus roaring:—Oh! Yoo-hoo! Oh! Yoo-hoo!—At some stage of event the minor of the women are having given chooks; this has emerged being alive. Those Africans hold over their heads fowls be shown that made of a theatrical, and have been active. On a whim knifes, by which women are started execute; and having chopped off fowls necks. Then roughly the women are tearing off parts of fowls feathers, and carcass wings.

Flora is scared—shaking:—Watching that incident, it's like being in a horror movie. Oh Lord!—

On a whim those women are started sipping blood out off deprived chooks. Then they jointly—are slowly spinning back and forth this fowls; which's having shattered here ghostly.

Given those women lifted in the air virtually lifeless chooks.

Once Flora comes into view—these women having violently shaken the fowls and yelling, by making eerie hums here. Flora is become scared, and feels in step as she befalls in one goes like being bewitched. In that case she is seeking of Mbeki's account of an occurrence that taken place here. Her eyes wide-open are stunned:—Mbeki, what is going on here? Why they're up roaring?—He murmurs is annoyed:—I advise to bow your head down. It's for your own good!—Flora is horrified; but rapt:—Why? What I've done wrong?—Mbeki murmurs into her ear:—As words spread by natives, who are believed that you, Flora bring bad luck in our community . . . !—

A bit later—till on flat terrain Flora has been given drink on hand by Candela on a wooden plate. As old woman offers it to Mbeki's wife with hold in, Candela grins, stretches a hand, and offers her:—Yes, take that!—Mbeki said:—Grandma offers you a drink, Flora, take it? Come on taste it!-

A sudden feeling of irregularity—Flora's head spinning: that image develops into blurry with flashes, seen those echoes are heard afar into rattle; with a flame, greater than before. Images of tongue with flame being dancing; as it seems be developed into hallucinations for Flora . . .

. . . Once Flora comes back to her sanity being bewildered and spotting a few men, who have arrived early, are standing aside, and they advent with a stare to Flora.

Where does she too have spotted those strangers. Next one of those guests comes near to Flora and without warning grabs her wrist; he then has launched an attack. Given they are trying dragging her away, towards sideway . . .

. . . As Flora starts pleading Mbeki for security; he is quite the opposite utters with amusement by contempt; and him being of critical eye; with mid intolerant deeds; he then is alleged. Mbeki in a firm says; is edgy:—Not a sole be desperate to put up with your company. I've tip you up that agreed by all of us: you bring bad luck—then you would either be executed or sold to a new Master! When comes down to it in the Afro Tribes ritual, and our way of life, Fleur!—By hearing of a shocking revelation, she couldn't believe it.

. . . So she is begging Mbeki, as looking terrified:—What you just said was a joke? This is a tale, isn't it? Defy me then, Mbeki? Let's hear it?—He turns aside to all says firmly:—No, it's not a joke, it's very serious. You're not longer my wife. Given that you have being sold to anew Master!—Flora tears drop down her face:—What are you talking about? We've got married. I'm your wife, back in my country, legally? Don't you remember, Mbeki?—She looks by fret in his eyes. Mbeki turns aside to an oppose side, where that public stands; without looking in her eyes. Flora is scared that aimed to cry:—You're a crazy man! Just now it is not as it was in past Century, just then of the Slavery time, when the people were sold, like commodity?—He in a deep, but strict voice declares:—You wrong Fleur! Slavery still exists! Cause I just sold you! You seems be ignorant that by my family owed a large sum of money to the Tribes Leader! For the time I was abroad The moment we had return from abroad

Master has claimed the pay back for a Loan. But my family was unable to give that amount back to him . . .

Mbeki stops; bobs his head to look at Flora; and spills out:—As for legality of our marriage it is unrecognized by the Law, and amid majority of our community, also in the Tribes: our marriage is illegitimate!—She remains be shocked—hearing of revelation as her eyes is wide-open.

Then Flora grabs purse out of Mbeki's hands—is ready rushing out. As she goes right pass that crowd, where he is standing with these rests of Manringa. Flora senses dumbfounded; it looks as if Mbeki has slammed her, in stomach with a lead pipe. Flora is sobbing; with plea to Mbeki, but being of fret:—I can't believe, what I have just heard? If this is ruled like that? You haven't got rights to decide on my behalf? This is my life!—Flora's directly backed off from her stand; a pace is indicating in despair:—Come home now, and give me back my Passport! I'll leave now, to return back to my homeland!—Seeing as Mbeki reacts with mirth; as murmurs to her:—I can't do it either! You see I am your master! I've the power over you! And I have sold your passport in company with you! It was a price I wanted pay to the rich Master for family's owned Loan!—He's head leaned aside; in grim says-so. Silence, and Mbeki continual:—You have not a clue as you nor longer my wife? Flora, my beauty, and stop defying, just go! Leave now with the natives! This is for your own good!—

By hearing Mbeki's proofs Flora began crying more like a mad; all at once figures out what has been said—that shocked, it seems her being naive to trust him.

Flora just now, has accepted wisdom:—Considering what has arisen? If I'll resist them, who emerge physically and muscular stronger men, as me being with weak parts; they're like the giants?—She takes a deep breath; then Flora thinks of more, be mute:—I haven't got a choice, to accept those strangers aver. Locals set up through their rules! That would be claimed me now for?—Winding up how to endure; also being a sign for Flora acts:—It could bring me more harm or worse of existent— endanger my life? Given not a soul that stand there; I can bet is unwilling too stand up for me, and protect . . .

Mbeki grins; next blows kiss towards Flora. So Flora has decided on the spot in the course of arisen she opts to.

Flora be placed identified a jeep that, she saw once when the guests had arrived a while ago, and which has driven along freeway . . .

So far Flora wants more guts pro her destiny. Her mind is racing fast; as she has sunk into a situation at this time. Acting she thinks:—What kind of demands a new Master has in mind? Given me have never met him or been dealings with natives.—

A bit later on a whim the jeep with Flora aboard stops swiftly; it occurs that one's car has blocked the way, which's made pro jeep up and of the crossing point to be blocked. So it seems traffic stops a whole convoy; as flash of headlights through speeding cars to be blindfolded. Follow the strangers of breaking lights are flashing into jeep. Flora chuckles by running at this point; is aware that it would-be safer fleeing now.

It has emerged that her hopes wholly faded away; Flora sits beside those foes in the front seat, which's started over. Then Jeep has driven away racing throughout a fractured road outside on freeway; that appeared be in poor state: by these gaps, which's felt hurting Flora's internal her organs, and the soft tissues.

CHAPTER 14

Later night in Meneliki's house she oddly scared; when the foes have placed she is in basement . . .

There she has found at least five other women, and one girl between them.

Flora peeks as the women are having got only blankets, which placed down and base being covered by a few rags, with no mattress as it felt roughly lay on the ground.

Flora just hoped is to get on a familiar terms with the other women; given she's seeking evidence that goes off, is tense. Flora:—What the hell happen to the women?—

In advance Flora starts a conversant with one amid those guards about apt pro Master Meneliki; by asking him over curiously:—Listen, what's master name? Do you work here as a guard? Don't you?—This first guard is arrogant in French:— Yes, I do. Our master was named after the country's former fame Emperor 'Menelik' . . .—, Flora looks as if is amazed, but ironic:—Really? What devotedly this ex-dictator Meneliki had, bravely done?—The guard raises his head; and slants; looks at Flora. He then turns talk in a different course:—What is your name? You're the new girl? Who's just arrived?—Flora seems be lost at sea:—My name is Fleur. Yes! But this is a mistake?—The first guard says firmly in French:—No mistakes! You're a new wife for master Meneliki! That's why you should know—historically Master raison d'être, was called of time-honored, when Menelik had gained independence for African Nation!—Kikwete stops, then gives Flora a little push to scare her off. A guard name Kikwete, who is ceased Flora with words of warning that, looming. The first guard is agitated, and talks in French:—And do not cause anymore trouble by asking! Go in the room, until you're called! Do you understand?—

Still in Meneliki's house—evening has arrived; Flora is lost in thought of those olden times, which have taken place in this country, where she was born . . .

Unexpectedly Flora has got intervallic due been called to go to another room. She follows the guard out throughout corridor, whose name turned out being Kikwete. He is at the age of mid or late thirties, muscular, and capable of any kind of cruelty. He is seemingly loyal to Meneliki; hearing Kikwete speaks French or wide-ranging dialects, by which those folks are interacting round Africa.

Entering the room fifteen minutes later, Flora peeks a man of middle age, who is also of an African look; sees like the rest, are turn out guards; as have worked as servants' for Meneliki.

. . . Proceed of feature of a middle-aged man, who's chunky, this man turns out—Master Meneliki. Given he is raring that looking bigoted at Flora; even if she has emerged tense. A Flora is asking, shyly:—Mr. Meneliki, why did you order me coming here? I'm a married woman! It's too late mid-night, now . . .

. . . Flora attempt to slip away behind the thugs; Meneliki stops her at once. He then clutches up his palms, in a deep voice. Meneliki in a brogue English:—You is my property and under my command! Fleur, you'll me obey!—He's response has made Flora insecure; see she is in subdued. Flora freezes being shy. Meneliki sees is in company with group of the guests, who are having emerged rebellious. When Flora tries resisting master is intend flee that weird bedroom, due to her has sensed tension.

As these rests of thugs have mutely exited; Meneliki then remains in bedroom. He turns as is facing Flora, this last being inert; but him liking a tête-à-tête with her . . . . There's Meneliki up a belt off his trouser and on a whim he smacks her! Follows by more smacks! Unleashing over Flora's upper joint; then over and onto her left upper limbs, of which she is hurting. She instantly falls down on a rug by layer of ground; it feels as Meneliki smacks! Throws punches at Flora over and over.

On a whim Meneliki climbs on top of her; his hands are ripping off Flora's clothes steadfastly; then is thrown its down. He pushed Flora that is rolling round; and over again on the floor. She gets aware immediately off he's intent to be raped. Flora is panting:—You bastard! Let me go! Go!—In a deep voice Meneliki is shouting at her:—Shut up woman! It best if you give up! Or you'll get punished for disliking it!-

Despite her resentment Flora has become exhausted; been in right mind. She is feeling head starts spinning; eyes amid a dim blur, then it has developed of more; and Flora loses consciousness . . .

As a result it's a lot of night raises Meneliki has raped Flora without her aware in so called—master bedroom, as she is being unable to defend her from cruelty and rapes.

One day Flora meets Meneliki in his front yard, but is running fast, before he sees her. But Meneliki and he's thugs unaware that she has heard during their talk; as hidden by tree-trunk, and he talks quietly, but firmly to one of his servers:—

Who of you're sedated meals? For this new, white girl?—He appointed one of thugs and lifts up his right finger. Then Meneliki commands him:—Carry on do that with catering!—

Flora is taken hardstand, what she has heard earlier.

So, those thugs abide Meneliki; caused Flora is became scared and stiff; when she mutely yields to herself. Flora with an attitude; pale:—How likely this has happened? Coz the thugs drugged me, and they've been inciting opium in chow? So of the effect, Meneliki has gained of my hallucination? Dear God help?—Hearing of that revelation Flora becomes watchful from this day on, when is in taking with serving her their cookery.

Be in basement against all odds Flora tried to keep firm mostly at night—and has resisted by Meneliki's demands in attempts of her getting raped often by him. On disclosure, she acts coherent, which would prevent her being bothered. Willfully misleading the brutes; she has made these thugs think is asleep, the sec they loomed in . . .

So often those thugs are closely kept an eye on her; more than for the other women; which are having established in basement, alongside Flora.

Over all calamities, exist and her being through, into the bargain Flora has suffered from hunger . . .

Yet with lots of slaps, bruises are left on Flora's body has predicted of no-win situation, where is found herself in. But Flora has pursued with a plan:—It's better than become a sex-slave for this monstrous master!—

Then overflowing of memory—she is New Haven University with clear image in her mind being into illusions through reminiscences: . . . Then after Mbeki has left; Friedman is in the hall, and supervising her on themes. She breathing deeply, and is involving him in talking. Friedman's head leaned aside:—Miss Whitmore I'm curious, how long you are two dating? It seems to me you've bonded only short time ago? Flora is dazed, in calm says:—No, Professor we're dating almost three months. I even left home to be with Mbeki in Dormitory.—She is breathing— seems being lost:—Yet fiscally be hard times for both of us. Still it feels like for Mbeki and me to be forever? What's your view about that, Professor?—He slants he's head, and is dazed:—Who knows? How long tough times could take? But fundamental here is what will lie ahead for both of you? Miss Flora, do you love Mbeki?—Flora in her place—is excited:—Of course, Professor! I'll do anything to be happy with Mbeki!—Stop. She is breathing deep, as if her being nosy, prolongs:—Why you're asking it Professor?—Friedman takes off glasses; gazes into her eyes, and puts it back:—But does he love you? Given love is a powerful thing! At times it could blind us up, and we'll befall to it! On the way loosing our merger!—A stop; he's taken breaths; looked her in the eyes, telling:—At some stage in one can end up either in heaven! Or to a point this could bring down to your knees and we will end up in hell! Yet, can we get back to rework a result of your exams? All points you get at my faculty; it's foremost to be focus?—She breathing out:— Oh, yes, most definitely, Professor!—Friedman looks her in the eyes:—what I am concern hereafter Miss Whitmore, that your insufficiency to study have gone down? I don't mean to bring about that's being the cause of your love for Mr. Manringa? I know for a fact that, you've got talent to be doctor of medicine. I followed your progress for few years. This is important for a success, as you Flora is graduating!—He stops, shakes his head, as if is unhappy, him lasting:—Now I'm not so sure that, you're so keen to make into a career, Flora?—She's restless, is panting awkwardly reacted:—You wrong, Professor! I want to become a Doctor! But my happiness is also important to me? Now, if you pardon me, Professor I am off! Must run!—Friedman takes his reading glasses off again; seen wipes he's lenses purposely of breaking silence. He looks in her eyes, and in calmly:—Miss Whitmore, I hope you've got a hint of my counseling here?—As Flora walks towards the door; her head slants prior exiting acts in response, is ironic:—Yeah, Professor! Neither I can by nor means!-

Back to reality: briefly Flora recalled has a chat; and that is given her enjoyment in midway of despair.

At least a week or two pass. Sees Flora is carried out dirty works, in front yard owned by Meneliki; but she does obey him and those thugs. She would devoid of be reminded; mostly by Meneliki. She is cleaning up pooh, after birds in patch, or down on land; and in a birds-cages of dirt free in the shit-hole out-of-doors. Apart from that Flora rakes for the hay or grassland, observe to be accessible close at hand here.

With another ten days goes by—and have seen Flora tried of tough working in Meneliki's yard, without her being reminded of—by anyone.

Later on in the course of times Flora would start call to mind: what she had learned by heart: parents and friends . . . Seeing as tears would pour from her eyes down the cheeks.

Back to reality: from nowhere a strange voice of dialect has struck Flora over her elbow ended on hip; this is brought her yet to reality. Hearing as one of Meneliki's guards' uproars and being brutal towards her, and yells in French:—Hey, you woman, don't stop! Go on working or you'll be punished!—

Once at dawn, Flora is waking up in basement, reminiscent be found back in parents' home. Without become aware of others, Flora starts recall, what her goals this time were, and murmurs to herself:—I didn't qualify up to my ranks-mates, then . . . ,—As a thing clicks for her:—Bingo!—

Be in Meneliki's basement, dawn—it's being miraculous, Power of Surviving comes to her through wisdom and out of space; that clicks with reflex. Flora would push herself to limit, execute flipsides; and back in front; she then in reverse—is landing through yoga . . .

Flora lost track of time! Despite lack of knowledge of their language; Flora invites the women for chat. Mishap she alike those women is seeking trusty. Be eager Flora talks:—I'm alike you're in captivity. I as you too hate violence, with a dead set against the muggers? Yeah? Do you understand, what I said?—So fed-up of misery, this has made her take upon doing yoga trainings.

Leopard

PART–IV

Risky Escape

CHAPTER 15

At dawn Flora is hard exercising in Meneliki's basement that, she would usual do on daily basis . . .

Suddenly she is hearing sudden din through approached of the echoes, which are from those shaky voices—obscured upheaval. Flora stops at once; in that case looks round for a hint to herself:—Okay! I need to stop now?—Then she listens watchfully; and is hearing those echoes from aside, where she spots the heavy door that would usually was locked up—just now it is turned up to be half-open.

Flora is worried:—What the hack? The door is open?—

A bit later Flora is determined leave basement, without being exposed by anyone.

. . . Without losing a second she warily comes across; where has looked round. First she starts fleeing stairway; climbs up; then passes aisle. Next Flora is coming up—towards a storeroom . . .

So she glances round; as to be ascertained. Flora exits . . .

She like a ghost:—Thanks God, not a soul saw me?—

. . . Yet Flora picks up blanket; covers her shoulders.

Next she is advanced to roomy; then passes through corridor. Flora is walking quickly, but felt worried.

As she turns to look round, and walks into storeroom, so she murmurs:—On every inch off travels I could hear my pulsing being soaring . . .—

She is passing through the bulky door; and leaving behind a dark access. A sudden stop of panicky, after Flora is hearing talks from a spot, where those thugs are in . . .

So Flora walks mutely, and looks for a place to hide in . . .

To her amaze a barrel emerged to be hidden in place for her:—I am in luck! I spot storage! There's a barrel to hide in?— Next she fast opens its lid—gets inner cask; folds down in the foetal position, and wraps herself up with cover.

. . . Sudden she freezes in a barrel, where she is surrounded by darkness.

Briefly those voices approaching close to hiding barrel, with Flora inner.

To her amaze by option those foes are having tried to pick up the cask. She feels her cask is lifted; her yell be heard dull, as those by few attempts have straggled to move it about; heard one thug's voice:—Listen, don't you think al fresco, as I feel the barrel we'd pick up, is gained some weight?—Next the second says-so:—Who cares? We just do our job!—The first thug then gets silent.

See those natives are begun shifting that barrel away; with Flora is of a tacit idea. As Flora thinks:—Perhaps they're taking my barrel upstairs?—

Now she is more relaxed; still nervously waits for those foes' deeds that are motioned, and shifting her outside . . .

Still in a barrel she is being positioned on hard surface of a lorry:—They placed my barrel at the rear of a car?-

She is relieved, when the lorry driving away; and yet accelerating.

As the lorry be driven—without cautious to be exposed, Meantime she tries open the lid:—The god demit lid does not open?—Lastly she is re-opened a lid to glance to al fresco, mindful of her lungs, and is taken with a full mouthful of air:—At last! Thank you Lord!—

So far Flora gets to break away, and be freed . . .

Given the driver is accelerating that, headed the track for who know where to . . .

Offhandedly of the lorry's travel along that main road . . .

If you're unaware of—this is existence of the ordinary Africans!

. . . Looking into driver's booth car-mirror, Flora views as two men are sitting inner, where one—steering. As the driver one time glances into car-mirror—there Flora's image be shown. And it's struck him; opt for telling his mate as he is uptight, so he says in French:—Look there is a woman at the back?— The second foe is seated in car booth near a driver, seems be jumpy:—No? It cannot be?—On the trot he spins round, and has caught Flora that browses he's eyes. A second is edgy, saying in French:—Jamal, now we're in deep shit! Meneliki deal with us?—

A tad later of driving sudden in midst-of-the-road sudden the car-driver is slowed down, and auto stops. Next see those foes are leaving car's booth; that madcap embarks upon her. Then the driver and another foe are jumping onto basket-body, and already having caught her. They are busy on the surface; seen Flora has resisted those rough hands, off anti their grips. As those foes lift the barrel with Flora in, and are taken her out, given they are tagging on that tied her up with straps.

Standby foes are having positioned Flora down on the base; where her being lying in back of the car. In spite of her yells of despair—and she is resisting those rough hands, which having ignored Flora's anguish being go on. One of those foe hits Flora, cause he is annoyed, and began blaring:—Oh, you're a real Bitch! You were thinking through your attempts, won't avoid to be caught by us?—

In due course of driving, the next stop by lorry is on motorway—and facing construct remind of storage there.

View those foes from car by now are—heeds they speaking

French, which have brought a side of relieve to Flora. In that case she boldly takes in hand the situation—to gain help from foreigners are footing. By hand gestures she is in despair; it seems her being eager to tell her story:—Excuse me! I hear you speak French? And so am I, gentlemen!—Strangers are shocked of her understood them.

They're listening; being coy, what she has told them in her despair a narrative . . .

Next one of them motions via his eyes to untie her. Once Flora has got untied off the ruler commands, with a stare one of foreigner looks at her as if is amazed, and refers to her bluntly in French:—Who are you? How you have entered the lorry? Where you're come from? Why did you . . .—, he looks at her—it rather seems be struck him:—I have exposed you? As I can see you're not a native here? Is it not true, woman?—

. . . A sudden major crop up there, which have affected Flora—is set in motion, without incompletion of her story . . .

From nowhere a vehicle is driving—shorten the distance between Flora stands and of those within the tail-chased auto. As she turns her head hear—bang with a hum, there is of width at the rear a car—approaching. Instantly a full ground rises; all there are in disarray by chased car. To prove she isn't wrong, then became upset; of forthwith Flora is begging stranger:—I know one of those thugs, in a car behind—they're Meneliki's P.A.! I was enslaved by him for some time! Please, help me?-

As Flora spins to side of these foes standing, which does driving at the rear approach. And Flora point to them; as is begging again:—I ask to help me escape? All of you must leave now, and to be united!—A foreigner is on edge:—Sorry, woman, we can't! We will be doomed . . .—

Her mind races fast; since she couldn't lose a second . . .

Turning aside—to her luck a car close to is placed over there. Without ado she is begum running towards the auto.

From the width she saw car-keys, which be installed into ignition. Flora inserts keys into ignition is on . . .

. . . Sudden one of those foes, who had, brought Flora here; rapidly opens the car's rear door, and jumps in front of passenger seat, where himself sits beside her. Flora puts the gear up, then smoothly is started the car. As she has pressed gas paddle, when saw the ignition is on. Flora's auto is begun driving off—by now speeding up.

Jamal is defying Flora—tried to stop, as distracted her from driving. He robustly is grabbing steering wheel out off her hands. He is stronger than her, an African well-built man. Jamal yells in French:—You're, Bitch! Slow down!—Sees a golden tooth is built-in his mouth; that's shown at what time he catchwords or would wide open a lot his jaws on.

. . . Flora often hits Jamal with her elbow onto his chest, so as to collapse or black him out. He stops for a sec. only if he is making new attempts to tussle her. But Flora is anti-thinking; seen her hand grabs hold of the wheel. Her foot id on: a gain to speed up; and she's increasing gas . . .

Then without warning one of those thugs in chased car; at the rear are having started shooting toward Flora's auto.

Flora is edgy, and yells in French:—Merde! It's become unsafe by an escapee? What are we going to do?—

. . . Jamal has curved round to absorb sight; he motions to a car at the rear. He pulls out a gun out of his holster; then is discharged it fast; he's emerged reloading it with bullets. Jamal's laid hands on gun; is ready firing from car-window . . . Those chasers are closing in; Flora quite the reverse is accelerating. Jamal sits beside be in vein; Buddy motions to:—Flora to speed up! You're and I need to stick as one . . .—, she looks doubtfully; but she doesn't hear him saying. So he yells back edgily:—What you were saying? I can't hear?—Buddy yells on top of his lung:—We're must stick here, as one! Speed up!-

After all has resolved he is become devoted to her. He's name is Buddy; this arisen of the man's real name—Jamal Korshal. So they two are forced to fleeing danger. Buddy is a local, in he is mid thirties; tall and muscular. But he acts by any form of violence if needed; on top him being a former marauder. She smiles:—I am Fleur for you I'll Flora! What about you?—Buddy by a nervy smile, talks of regret:—My real name is Jamal Korshal. As for you I'll be Buddy, okay?—She agrees; and nods her head, all at once motions her head aside without losing the track, then:—Okay! That's a deal, Buddy!—But Buddy is curious, asking her:—What's you doing here, girl?-

So far Buddy is in the position, when he began shooting. Then Buddy is edgy, as he turns aside:—It's emerged be odd, but a risky ordeal to escape for us both? I'll back you up, Fleur!—At that point sees Buddy is shooting now from car-window; and is carrying on firing towards Meneliki's thugs' . . . ,

. . . This chased car instead—is matching with double act be driven fast, and on full-speed. When Flora checks car's speedometer, is shown—85km . . . , 87 . . .—keeps climbing up.

On motorway a sudden stop this time lorry is in front of a build being reminded of bulky erect storage near.

Those foes from lorry meantime—are having interacted in French. Heeds they have spoke French that brought side of relieve to Flora. She boldly takes in hand the situation: to gain help from foreigners, who are footing; by hand gestures, it seems she's being eager to tell them her story is anxious:— Excuse me, gentlemen! I hear you speak French? And So am I!—The foreigners are shocked that she can understand them. They're listening; being coy; that she has told about her runaway . . .

Seen one of the foes motions via his eyes clues to untie her. Once she gets untied off ruler commands, with a stare he refers to Flora bluntly, which's inquiring her directly. Foreigner is amazed, and began talking in French:—Who are you? How you entered this lorry? Where are you come from? Why did you . . .—He then:—I've exposed you! I see you not a native here? Isn't it true, woman?—Without incompletion her story of event; Flora is set in motion; cause as it having affected her by a major occur . . .

From nowhere a car is driving by to shorten the distance between Flora's stand and of those of a tail-chased auto.

As Flora turns her head to bang with a hum; there's of width at the rear a car is approaching . . . . Instantly a full ground rises; all there are in disarray by chased car. To prove she was not wrong and become upset; of forthwith Flora's begging:—I know one of the thugs, who in the car behind— they're Meneliki's P.A.! I was enslaved by him for some time! Please, help me?—

Flora's mind races fast, but she couldn't lose a second . . .

As she spins to face side of this foes standing, and is approached by driving at the rear; as she point to them; when she is begging them:—I ask you're helping me to escape? All of you must leave now, and to be united!—The stranger is reacted:—Sorry, we can't! We'll be doomed . . .—

By turning aside, to her luck a car near to is placed.

. . . Next Flora is running toward the car. From the width she sees car-keys be installed into ignition. Flora swiftly inserts keys into ignition; and next she is started the auto. Flora urgently but smoothly is started the car, and driving off . . .

A sudden one of foreigners, who had brought Flora here—rapidly opens car's rear door; and jumps in front into the passenger seat; where he sits beside her. She puts the gear up; and has pressed gas paddle; see ignition here is on; and her speeding up.

Jamal tried to stop is anti Flora—distracted her from driving. He robustly is grabbing steering wheel out off her hands. He is stronger than Flora; an African well-built man. Jamal yells in French:—You're, Bitch! Slow down!—Sees a golden tooth is built-in his mouth; that's shown at what time he catchwords or would wide open a lot his jaws on.

Flora often hits Jamal with her elbow onto his chest, so as to collapse or black him out. Jamal stops for a sec. Given that he is making new attempts to tussle her. But she anti-thinking; seen her hand grabs hold of steering wheel. Flora's foot on: A gain to speed up, and she is increasing gas . . .

Without warning one of those thugs in chased car; at the rear are having started shooting toward Flora's vehicle.

Flora yells be edgy in French:—Merde! It's become unsafe by an escapee? What are we going to do?-

. . . The chasers are closing in; Flora's accelerating. Jamal is seated beside, be in vein—motioned for her to speed up:—You're and I need to stick as one . . . ,—Flora looks doubtfully;

but she doesn't hear him saying, she yells, anxiously:—What you were saying? I can't hear?—Jamal then yells on top of his lung:—We're must stick as one! Speed up!—Jamal has curved round observe the sight, he motions to this car at the rear. He pulls out a gun out of his holster, and has discharged it; as he is emerged reloading it with bullets. Jamal's laid his hands on gun—ready firing from car-window to chasing car . . .

After all has resolved, he is become devoted to her. He's name is Buddy; this arisen of the man's real name—Jamal Korshal.

So they're two forced to fleeing danger. He is an African local; in he's mid thirties; tall, muscular. Jamal could act by any form of violence if needed; with an advantage him being a former marauder.

Flora makes acquaintance:—I'm Fleur from US! What about you?—Buddy grins; talks of regret:—My real name—Jamal Korshal. As for you I'll be Buddy, okay?—She agrees; motions her head to aside without loses the track. Flora with a wide smile; nods her head:—Okay! That's a deal,

Buddy!—As he is curious:—What's you doing here girl?—

. . . So far Buddy is in the position, when starts shooting. He is edgy; thus turns aside:—It's emerged be odd, but a risky ordeal to escape for us both? I'll back you up, Fleur!—Buddy sees is already shooting from car-window; and is carrying on firing towards Meneliki's thugs' . . .

. . . This chased car is matching with this duo be driven fast and on full-speed. When Flora checks speedometer, it's shown—85km . . . , 87 . . .—keeps climbing up.

Meantime those thugs in the chased car, accelerating are pursued Flora with her new mate's in their car, with the intention to catch that duo. A first chaser amid two in car is barreling towards North, for the Plateau. Buddy stops. Given that one of his hands is atop; with a second hand he clings to steering wheel. Then a second chaser talk is angry. A second chaser yells; be edgy:—They are going away fast! But this Bitch is holding the tracks!—

As next Flora checks car-mirrors sudden views; where those two in car-tailed at the rear are having ensued the chasers, and they already driven in closer . . .

Buddy still is frantic; and he logically suggested:—They are speeding near and chased us in the car in back! Those thugs are closing in! Look they're not far-off; you hold on to steering wheel, and press on gas?—She yells, eyes on alert:—Copain de regard (d'apparence) . . . ,—Flora's pal Buddy disrupts her; aloud as is predicting ahead. Buddy points a hand on the road:—Go faster! Don't go off as to be smashed by the chaser. I will able to slaughter those thugs! Nor fear, Flora!-

A sudden explosion boom! Echo is heard. As this duo have observed from wide space; where ruins flew up in the air and beyond. Seen ruins then and there have left scrutiny on or after the blasts in breach of grey dust; this has flown up . . .

Flora sits beside Buddy is edgy; as the car takes them to highway, after hearing an awful blast! Explosion! Boom! Follows: a second is massive Blast! Impact! Bang! View garage edifice shakes by slow motion, gets rocked; then hits the ground; metal be destroyed. Flash of light in a blitz. A blast trails, and spits; is faded dim through indicator of smoke. A Flora murmur is scared:—What's up with the folk's? As traits standing a yard, only two of them have left behind alive?—Her mate with a stare at those ruins; which's spread out into less of envisage on distance of visible smog. In Buddy's view accident with seals of horror; so he tugs Flora's sleeve. He is grim, says in French:—Listen, girl turn around (go back) and throw one glance. Since the view is terribly poor, ahead!

. . . She makes a speedy turn back; given is seized through stirring wheel; instead reducing speed by cause of riots. It's lacking of Flora's attention to those are chasing them at the rear. In time inch by inch she has shorten gap between hers car—against those thugs' motor; so that she is accelerating.

Buddy wildly pulls of waistband a spare gun; as outlines through car's windshield; and he starts shooting towards chasers are on flames; even if latent get off target.

In due course of the battle through a cross fire they are fighting forcefully; given that both having extremely backfired to rivals. Flora glances that sudden her travel mate has been injured; she . . .

So Flora directly suggests to Buddy, who's by now become her new ally; so she is told her view of the situation. Flora tails fast, but is intense:—Listen to me, Buddy! Let's swap our place (seat)! Allow me to be in charge of a chaos. I'll discharge, as shoot from your gun at foes, pronto?—Even if Flora was untrained, as holds steering wheel; as her eyes are fixed straight to glance on the road; and she says-so is fretful:—I've not been involved in a real fight! Nor had I joined such danger to get through revenge!—She's kept backfiring; but she never got caught into a cease-fire, infinitely it's safe for her own defense. Buddy grins:—Come on, be brave. You can deal with it!—She sees to Buddy position his gun into her hand. So she has learned fast, which's intended of a situation known-how. See she is firing gun straight—on target. By reloading gun-magazine full with bullets, she paved way into firing position, and is shooting to defend both of them, through the car-window towards the tailed-car.

. . . So far exchange of fire, which Flora has caught up stuck between both sides—defying Meneliki's thugs. Flora is edgy, and asking him in French:—A clash against thugs, who pursued their god demit plans; in one go escalating whole effect. Buddy is edgy:—We're as to be cut off?—

A gap between Flora and Buddy anti the thugs in chased car—shrinks, yet widens; the double act is estimating their aim; and being getting less edgy; to be driving of non-stop through the wildness. Buddy reacts:—Look, Fleur we accomplished! Firing of guns, have now subsided?-

. . . Flora beside Buddy has yet driven out of reach. The duo act flat of is unable spotting chase-tailed car as it's vanished.

Flora's car is heading toward wilds; via windshield they are sighting a vast herd amid gazelles afar inaccessible; which having been sprinting on speed. In-groups gazelles are doing in a way of galloping; by which would match to Flora and Buddy's vehicle in speeding.

Flora be in awe; as she talks to him in French:—You, know something Buddy, it looks as if a beast chased that elegant Herd among the gazelles . . .

He is tensed:—Probably. We'll never know?—Buddy leans his head; by his eyes signs up to her. As he warns: Now, be at alert on the road! We're not yet out of the woods! This is awful speed of gazelles; as the living things are made attempt on winning that race through their sprint.

From car-window Flora gazes at parallel side, where peeks far-off at least two-dozens of single group of elephants are into hard-walking. While these mammals—rushing of somewhere.

In stages of runaway within plateau Flora in car's sit beside Buddy, who is grasping for victory—defy these chasers aim in a car. It's ideal for this duo is to be ahead of chasers; which have disappeared from view . . .

Buddy observes; and points a hand to:—I can't see their car? Now we're driving, bias hanging on for at least over twenty minutes!—Flora is convinced:—OK! Buddy, are you positive?— He responds:—Yes, I'm, we lucky to vanish.

At dusk Flora alongside Buddy are glimpsed across gap of highland. There comes into view adjoin region of environs—of African natural world.

First stop Buddy has made near hill; remote of Plateau. Flora's mate points he's hand and letting know; tips her up. Buddy points a hand on a side:—Look there at peak a sole surface is set of like a cave! We're in luck! Here's our chance too hide inside, and to rest?—Flora interim observes—nods her head:—If say so its good enough. I see you're familiar with the broad site here? I'll just follow, wherever you're in . . .—

They're both having begun climbing on top of that hill.

Within hours of darkness this duo found on spot that have bordered of a cave alike. That double act has made out their mind; as to be settled within the cave without delay; by urgency. Buddy is content:—That's just the right place for us to sit put, for a while?—Flora is eager, bends to show:—Yes! I also have brought Aid pack to heal us! Because you see we badly need it . . .

At night near the plateau—this duo is in a cave, having suffered fatigue. So as to let slip parts of that double act's limbs are aching from earlier encounters, spotted cuts and bruise on their skins. A hot wound bothered him in part being of his soft tissue and at his collarbone. See to be aimed for her cuts minor bruises. Flora shows up an aid kit:—Look Buddy, let me make you a temp bandage, which will give you relief from the pain!—Buddy turns head aside to her:—How? Do you have medications?-

CHAPTER 16

At dawn Buddy and Flora are sleeping in a cave. Suddenly strangers have disturbed their siesta. From the time when those thugs from chased car have formed a circle; view they are footing over Flora and Buddy's eyes. Given he and she are watched by the thugs; which's having seized barrel of a gun toward Flora and Buddy's heads, as both equally are targets. Flora is rapidly up on her feet. Buddy whispers; slants head to:—Keep closer, I'll be backing you up!-

Sudden a thug hits, and Flora falls down on the stony ground. She is resisting as pulls lead up; and hits this thug into his groin:-"Ouch!"—Spots she is thrown punches at this thug; by defiance, an enemy drops his gun down on the ground . . .

As a foe jumps on his feet—comes to blow against Buddy. See next one of these thugs whips a gun off Buddy's hand,

and repeatedly slams this last one's hand—against the edge. A stylish rotary motion between Buddy and this thug from a reverse spin. Then another thug jumps in; and hits Buddy with an elbow into his throat; when hooks-on, and knocks between this last one's ankles in the mid-air. This thug is flipping in part, and sending Buddy's gun flying up in the air . . .

It seems those thugs haven't foreseen a tough battle from

Flora and Buddy. In the end those thugs are started loosing patience with Buddy; and this same from Flora's resistance too . . . The muggers with offense from behind to Buddy's head of a sweeping block; he is defiant capturing this thug's limb in an arm-lock.

. . . The gunfire goes wide, shattering in a urinal. These have got to hurt Buddy; so this last one is dropped his gun down.

See a hasty trap is set by one of the thugs is removed a gun and shooting; sees a shell flown straight to Flora . . . But Buddy peeks; a jump over he covers Flora and is shielding her.

Buddy looks with wide-open eyes to enemy, and attempts to hold his balance; after he was being shoot down . . . Firing squad of bullets finally guns down. He falls down; but is trying to shift away; while clings to life. The last shell is flying into Buddy neck, intended that finish him off. He stops in stages of he's last breathe; and weaves his head towards exit; as in his eyes are a fair warning for help. He whispers in French:—They killed me, Fleur. But my warning—you must be on alert!—He is wheezing:—Cause you intend to be drawn in ahead by more danger! Be careful.—Buddy stumps by last words—against lucid through his final breathing; he freezes by death posture.

But for Flora Buddy's words meant that, he's an honorable man, who lies dead. She mumbles, as weeps:—Despite of Buddy's odd deeds, when the two of us were in conflicts . . . ,—her gasps deepen:—In the past he was a marauder! But he had shown of his honorable side by a last favor to let me live on! I'll never forget you, Buddy!—She sheds and wipes tears that rolling down her cheeks.

The situation made her ensued to be careful of drawback.

Without loosing a second Flora is fleeing a cave like in full swing, in an attempt for her to stay alive . . .

On exit she is running away to barren spacious tract to find help; or for her too hide in from the muggers . . .

Flora is running—secluded; but she has underestimated the thugs opt; they're following her at the back. Flora is running forward; given her being barefooted that, bears pain of rocks round.

Flora:—I am at a complete loss without a twig, where to run? But I bear each stone under my soles; but the sharp items of shrubs are killing me? I would try to put off side inept?-

Saw next Flora falls down to the ground—with strength of will is forcing her to mount back. Then she is up—and running madly.

Since Flora's along the African plateau it's amazed of flash in face, which made lift up her head. There's an image that sparked from above; off soil be rose a vast trunk of well-known African Acacia tree.

Flora loses her speed; which images have captivated her eyes. While her being chased behind by Meneliki's thugs. Flora alludes:—I have a choice either climb up a tree? As it has vast capacities that may help me hide inside?-

A sudden sight on top of the tree is a Leopard that has looked atop of acacia's branch down to Flora. Her breath is caught in; as she froze of fear. A leopard is watching her from above. In the beat looks as if it wants to jump down in alacrity to attack her. Maybe this wild animal has picked her for its prey. Flora became scared:—What I'm going to do now? The wild leopard can kill me? It wants to stuff itself with a human flesh? Or the thugs will get me, and I would be enslaved again? God help?-

. . . Flora's apt and gets stop by one of the thugs, by which a barrel is started shooting on gorgeous, but a dangerous animal.

One of those thug's gunshots has missed his shot only by inches, and scaring the killer cat. So that heard in the leopard's turn is of:—Ar-ar! R-r-r!—This killer cat is in motion; then jumps off tree down on the ground. This beast well under way partly soars; this beast runs fast. A leopard has left the tracks—is made dust through its sharp jagged claws.

Flora is kept racing away from those thugs via the same path; just where the leopard has run prior. In spite of those thugs are looming and lagging behind to catch her with out crying woes; but she keeps running fugitively. While Flora thinks:—Buddy's dead. Yet I'm in danger. I am inept to shield myself against muscular built men. How those thugs and Meneliki are going react toward me? If I will be recaptured?—

In the long run those thugs are succeed; seeing they're yet having caught up with Flora; in difficult situation to her.

. . . Sudden hit by one of the thugs who's struck her hard below; this has ended on her ankle. On impulse of the thug's hit be awfully spread over her narrow parts; that resulted Flora is falling off downhill on the ground; as being unconscious . . .

Flora came back to senses that a self's hand is lightly slapping her face. She hears one of the thugs is called her name; that emerged being guard Kikwete. It struck her bluntly by his remarks. Kikwete by disdain; in French:—Oh, that's for you Bitch! You've thought pretty that we will go away without a catch? Then you have deceived yourself, Bitch! Flora retorts:— Shit! To you pretty, and all of you're sickening Bastards! Kikwete in French:—You'll be punished for that, Fleur!—Without losing a second Flora spins by lightning maneuver, knocks out a silence pistol off Kikwete's hands. But he drives her to the surface ground in rotation. Flora's head dropped; Flora is stuck between Kikwete's boots; given this last is sitting on the can that blankly looks down at her. Kikwete pulls out ropes of his pocket; and applied zip-strip like handcuff, as to secure her wrists. He tags on; and ties her legs up equally. Flora is sagging into submission . . .

At dusk Flora is in the basement, but she doesn't know about it: a moment or two pass since she's awaking, but her physical parts still being immobilised, because bodily parts are mêlée of these with ropes. And so she starts to experience great pain all over the parts of her internal organs from these cuts and bruises of some wound too, but she doesn't pay much attention to that. Instead Flora looks around on encircled area, and became mindful—her be situated in a gloomy room by a place similar to basement, that she reflects:—I was in here early on? . . .—

When Flora tries to move her arms along with legs, as she finds the motion parts of hers being tied up with ropes. To hers luck the foes her mouth have exposed that Flora being able to breath. So she began through its way often intake gulps of air, until her breathing is stabilized. Next she tries to move through her muscular parts. In spite of Flora's strength, it's being beyond her power to unfasten these ropes, and to brake free from it . . .

When she glances round the space, where is finding sharp objects that having handiness for her attempt to escape.

From distance she has spotted a screw-driver, surround by other gadgets in the toolshed. Next Flora is begun fast shifting towards the item that sited over there yonder. Still it has not been that easy at first, she's distorted off foetal pose into uncurling up her legs, by constantly moving them, at the same time as using muscular parts of her legs and arms—moving these objects simultaneously . . .

In time Flora feels that her wrists have felt sore, but for next travels she is begun step-by-step by rolling and turning over to intervallic gauge, alike a ball by the length of the base, while on that she is gently sloping, which has caused her great pain. Flora regularly turns round over the base—with short rupture that separating her from aims. In that case she would bring to temporary halts in-between her attempts. In the long run Flora is silently drawn closer within reach of that gap, where she seen a screw-driver to be positioned. She tried barely to place that aimed gadget to trimly cutting off these knots and untie ropes. After few attempts Flora is passive; be at a halt she couldn't reach this tool. Then with use part of her forehead she throws it down, and object falls down into her lap. Except how hard she was trying place a screw-driver, even being pushing herself to the limit as to cut off ropes, or at least unfasten her hands which tied, but her attempts—unusable.

A long time passes; when Flora gradually starts react to exhaustion—then bit by bit she is fallen asleep.

Sooner or later, one has come and disturbed Flora's dream in the basement.

This one starts opens front door, where also being heard sound from intensified vibration of highness is coming from remote. She wakes up slowly to the reality—Flora's voice made echoes:—I'm not aware, if it's day or night?—While she is half-asleep, but her mind has raced fast withstand all risk, which she needs facing yet to be. So she is breathing deeper, and come what may—cover up position of her figure. Though her body-parts are still tied up with ropes, and she felt the foes have removed her out of basement.

Fired Flora's despair is briefly befalls blindfolded up her eyes that she meant to be hidden from view. She is unable see, whereabouts her be supposed to reallocate.

Flora senses being placed on hard surface of basket-body. She is thinking: I'm sure on one thing: I have been used as a target by those thugs . . . They might send me to a new place?—Those foes consider untying her. Next one of foes is removed blindfolds out of her eyes; but she has become exposed towards sunlight. In the truck near Flora is spotting odd mass of supply, which is covered with jumbo; be made of wooden boxes.

The truck speeds up with non-stop down the road; yet she peeks half-a-dozen or more amid foreigners; who usually are native Africans or from close locality?—Flora is lacking of Gen. Language; and she is guessing:—Where they have headed for, possible to the highway?—

The minute truck comes in to stop; a heavy door becomes ajar with obscurity. The stripe, which have blindfolded Flora been removed from her eyes, where near harbor pier . . .

Given that thugs are pushing those captives out, Flora is counted up amid; by exiting she has stuck between them.

As the driver unbolts track's door; those captives are stepped out.

A yak start between muggers; hearing their interaction Flora is inept to understand the language.

Soon muggers are collecting those captives that stepping through—and over Flora is being seated. Those muggers are ruling—having treated her in the same way as the rest of detained. See muggers: money change hands.

Later on those thugs are having engaged in the process for countdown amid those captives; with Flora tot up as to be glanced . . . One man in charge in a commanding voice:

—You people, pay attention to our ruling! All of you're getting off truck, faster!—Thus Flora is exposed too inept, has felt out of action; given of arisen that she deprived of a chance to escape now. Flora falls down like android; be robotic following those captives, who are too marching ahead of her towards . . .

Elephants at Dusk

Ship

PART–V

Perilous Voyage

CHAPTER 17

Remark—a vessel be positioned in front of Port Bay . . .
Later that day amazingly in front of Flora's eyes has
emerged a view: with that panorama of a grand vessel there.

Given that Flora didn't have retained travels ID he asks her.
The second man in charge says in English; be nosy:—Woman,
where's your passport?—Flora reacts be shy but tense:—I don't
have passport with me, it's missing. My husband has it . . .—

A sudden arrays, as Flora's mind is racing fast:—If I shut
up then I can fix on what is best for me to do? And if I take the
cruise on this ship and fleeing Africa far? Until I'll swim closer
to shores of my homeland?-

In Port Bay prior boarding the ship Flora attempts to escape.
Flora is spotting a car from a distance; that hasn't left yet: that
she makes an effort to flee again.

Then Flora is made an attempt; and begins running toward the car. On the way Flora is roaring franticly:—Please, somebody help me! Take me to the Embassy . . .—, But she is stopped by one of that unruly. Hatefully one of them hits Flora over mid-parts of her bodily backsides; so that painful reality made her cease a plan, if she just wants to be live? She lastly subsides, and gave in.

. . . At the end of the day the ship steadily is sailing off

—navigate passing through port; so that those sailors, who have being giving orders into the crossing.

For Flora has spotted crowds, which are brought aboard, amid foreigners and white folks; who be placed on deck . . .

Flora tries speaking to those captives, is lacking of knowledge of the language.

From this moment on, Flora has aimed to herself:—I must obey them without doubt! With the lot that destiny might throw upon me!—

. . . A few days pass of travel by water, Flora is walking on upper deck.

Sudden she is hearing shrill crashes; where are seeing these sailors running back and forth in a turmoil.

Next an incident has grown into exchange of gunfire. One from the crew has got drunk; which's begun a rampage with others from that crew. This one from ship's crew emerged rioting; the rest of them turn against each-other. Given a self is being shooting on another sailors—looming through them has begun shooting. After firearm is shot; in the past few minutes saw one of that crew was injured.

Flora senses unsafe if bear wellbeing of sailor's harm; given that the man is bleeding. Still this sailor has shown signs of him being in opposition to Flora.

A sudden yell from aside amid one among those captives there. Jean-Luc talks loud in brogue English:—I am a doctor! This man needs medical help, urgently!—Flora couldn't be heartless toward injured one, and she boldly exclaims to one of the sailors, who are present. Flora's urgent, but loudly:—I am doctor too, I'm here! Let me help to treat his wound?—

These sailors go round to glance at Flora. Then one amid those sailors acts in respond. Abdullahi in a peculiar look:—Okay! Hey you're two make a bandage for him!-

Soon, Flora seeks to help this captive to operate on the sailor's wound. A traveler has removed a bullet out off sailor; seen cuts been with pattern on bleeding traces into open wound of, that flesh being spotted on sailor's skin; this practice be done with Flora's assistance. The traveler looks be shocked:—So, you're a Doctor too?—Flora looks around, be scared:—Well, not quite, but getting to!—Traveler shakes with his upper limbs:—How's that? I'm Jean-Luc, what's your name?—Flora beams, seems is excited:—I did study in med school. My name is Fleur, but I have been called Flora!-

Suddenly the ship's Captain prevents them from talking, says firmly:—Hey, you're two, shut up! Do it faster his dressing! Get out of here. Go down in cabin, woman!—In the care of the captive, Flora has placed a bandage that covered a man's wound. She offers under captive orders the injured one medicine; intend for subsiding his pain.

The next morning Flora awake is hearing noise. She comes close to access. Her ear puts to the door, and hears that a self is on foot just passing through her cubicle.

Shortly Flora climbs staircases; and appears on ship's upper deck. When she turns round; looks on other side, at the man that is footing, who has prior given his consent to assist with bandage on the injured sailor. The skipper is of Northern African look, as his skin being lighter, metamorphoses practical not older compare to the rest of that crew; and hearing him talking in a brogue English.

Flora is clear on one thing coercing bears in her mind:-

To consider so far I have nothing to loose, one-way or the other?—Flora boldly advances the skipper; as endures too think:—As this ship didn't enter open sea, yet?—

In a difficult situation she's grown to be daring; cause now is a chance for her—so she bravely approaches one, who's Captain to yak. She speaks of guts:—Excuse me, sir! I heard you were spoken English, before?—He smirks; is saying with an accent:—Yes, I have and doom!—Though his expression has suddenly changed; and he says-so:—How come, you ended up on here?—Flora is taken aback:—What do you mean? Ended upon here?—He is heated; but curio:-What the Hell you're doing here? How it's arising you're ended up on my ship cruise? What is your name, woman?—Her look is of desperation:—I'm Fleur. I was detained by folks, who had fetched me here. Before I have tried to escape, so as to find the Embassy from my homeland . . . ,—Flora then stops; desperately looks in his eyes. As she solicits is begging this ship's captain:—I've to return back on shores! And fly to my homeland?—A skipper stops her; smirks and alone speaks with a biting wit:—I see. And so, what you are doing here? On African shores? How did you get in this country? And who did it?—Flora barges in; by a nervy reacts with a respond to him; and looks as if be anxious:—Back in my homeland I married an African citizen.—She stops to breathing in. After our arrival here, he had changed; and was rejecting me as a wife . . . ,—Flora is breathing deeply, and is telling more:—Later my husband sold me to new master for he's family owed loan . . . ,—She continual—of her brutal lives in captivity, and foremost a myth of her escapee . . . Flora has made clear to him with a story of her life. Then she is begging the Captain:—Could you let me get off ship on the next stop? I'll get a valid passport in Embassy, and return back to my homeland?—Abdullahi smirks, shakes his head:—I can't do it. You see a master owed you're! You were wrong, to break free? Given you have been sold. And your role is to oblige Master, not rejecting him? As for a punishment: your fate will be decided?— Flora is with a stare of shock:—What you're saying? I can't grasp you? It's the twenty first century, and slavery had long gone! We're civilized people with progress of high Technology that humans creating ranges to advance!—Abdullahi stops her:—You wrong again! Think about?—She looks him in the eyes as if being pleading him. Above all Flora is tense, reacting firmly:—Not a sole have rights to be sold, like animals or kind of things!—But he cuts her short:—You wrong again! Think, here in Africa the Law is different!—Abdullahi points up to a shelf, where Koran is:—Above all Shiite Law, by origin a lot to be privileged for us!—Abdullahi stops; turns be nasty, and in harsh words; alleged:—You're under my orders! Don't forget you in our hands!—Flora is mocking him:—How can I? You wouldn't let me?—He is jumpy; in a command tone:—I can do with you, suchlike I would desire!—At that time he starts to tell his story:—Once ago I have studied abroad Higher Education. So, don't give me a shit talk! I would either kill you or do with you anything I could wish, cause I owe you, from now on!—Abdullahi looks her over, as she stands be at a complete lost. He with an approval has uttered, as being spotting her. He is obsessive:—See if you'll suit my whim! Even with your wild character . . . And until I decide on your fate!—He's recurring; tells more:—Do you get a hint? Your name's Fleur,—she stops him, be scared:—Why you're playing games Cat and Mouse with me? If you have just told me that, you studied at College in a Western nation? What I did wrong here or corruptly? And too you're most of all, sir?—The captain at first smirks. Then his expression alters to a stern look. As he curves down, as moves closer to Flora's face. She hears him shouting. Abdullahi is in a deep raging voice:—Not me personally, but your people and I mean white had made living Hell for our people in the past! You're Whites for century had in slaved; exploited us, mainly those blacks! All from round Africa . . .—, He gives a smirk; look at her from top and down; dull:—Yet how does it feel?

What's like to be a Slave? And in Hell? Hey!—Flora stops him; as if is offended:—For your information, I've never thought of Africans to be slaves. Secondly, I have neither humiliated Africans, nor lesser than at all the diverse Races! Above all the African culture! I fell in Love with an African man!—Flora is breathing heavily; and continual being avid:—In the end I've went after my husband inhere, too adopt your cultural belief and build a live in Africa. I was hoping too become one among your way of life; as gain to be citizen!—Abdullahi is begun laughing; talks in deep voice:—Ha! Ha! Ha! Come again? You're amazed me! It seems my dear that, you're ignorant, where you should be taken away for?—He alters to grim:—Firstly, it isn't my birth country! You've got all wrong, mixing me with other black Africans!—He stops, smirks; then is prolonged:—That's just how you're having reacted to my meaning of vigor . . .

CHAPTER 18

At dark Flora is standing in access strip—listens in close proximity to her cubicle be heard one's stepladder . . .

Suddenly she hears someone roams over ship's deck base.

Then a self starts descent off staircases.

And Flora is rushing in a cubicle. Inwardly she sits down on narrow-gauge bunk bed.

As the trait draws near her cabin; steps in first knock. Flora pulls up her head facing this same skipper, with whom she has got earlier, into spat. She spots that he is wore loose; just as he's eyes with a piercing sharp stare—are ardently fixed in a flash of her. Skipper's lips quiver on his face shown of bursting. Flora by sense of the man's enmity; of goose-bumps upon her skin. View a he straightens his posture; and comes within reach of her; as he's deed is conceited. She is grown being alarmed. Abdullahi smirks; says be ironic:—Well, Fleur, you know what I think? You and I didn't finish talking about things?—She's with a stare; talks slowly:—What do you want to talk about? Before you plainly told that my authority isn't intend. Also you just said that I belong to you, as a thing. Isn't it true, skipper?—He looks her in the eyes; smirks, and is revealed angrily:—My name is Abdullahi Riesa . . . !—He stops, and sneers. Looks in her eyes, he then tells more:—Secondly, you're right! Now, don't forget you're on my ship! And I can do with you whatever thing I want! Would you like to know, what mine desire is, Fleur?—But she cuts him short, and alleged guardedly her is cynical:—So, you do have a name, than? I didn't invite you here. And if you don't mind to leave? Cause I need get to sleep! Anyhow, it's late night now . . . ,—Abdullahi disrupts her; and is saying with an annoying voice; additionally in a bad humor:—I came here to get what I desire! And you'll give it to me, by obliging! If not, I hope you probable realize by now, that bunch of my crew you're dealing with, Fleur? We aren't joking!—She keeps calm; then in tensed voice she's alleged:—And I hope you know that I'm a married woman! I did tell you before, didn't I, Mr. Riesa?—Instead he smirks; says be edgy:—I don't give a toss!—The skipper then natters in sardonic tone, as with a stare into her face:—But your husband rejected you? You have told me so earlier! With my spare gifts, now I owe you! Only

I've power over you! Cause I'm your Master!—He stops; looks at her, smirks; and Abdullahi tells, as is burst:—So I don't need to ask for your consent to do with you such like I desire! But if you, pretty, Fleur is constantly rejecting me for your luck won't be so optimistic!—Next he grabs her hand and tried to kiss her. He is emerged being stronger compare to her; when he throws her down on the bunk-bed; yet his desires clearly is established—to force him upon her.

A few seconds later Flora is pushing Abdullahi closer to electric rosette, where some inches from bed she has spotted a sharp metal point, by which those tiers up; and she clings to it. But Abdullahi is on guard as too spots a sharp metal; and shield himself with a 9 mm gun; and being shown off it up in the air from he's fasten to lose her balance; moves from behind. Abdullahi breaths in; deep voice:—Fleur, you will give up!—Be heard for her exhale:—Le-let me, go-go-oh! You bastard!—Abdullahi's dull eyes, in avid says:—Oh, you're a real bitch! Fleur, if you're unwilling to abide me?—Even if Flora does a spin round to get into anew position up front; but she misses skipper's hit; that he is now up on his feet; and starts with offences against her. Given that Abdullahi is shaking his gun in the air; he then attempts by offenses towards Flora. Except she disrupts him from talking, is fussy:—Abdullahi, why don't you shut the fu** up? I'm not scared! OK?—He is dogged:—You not? Fleur, you know, you one wild, wild, beautiful thing! Flora with disgust:—Yeah? I couldn't be glad! Crawling on your whipping of a helpless woman? Want me to beg you, asshole? Fu** that!—

If you're unaware it's a wild clash amid Abdullahi and

Flora; that keeps her head above water; as for her not get raped . . .

Abdullahi executes a neck fold; grabs Flora from behind with his free hand, and circles her neck's collar with hair into grasping. As he starts to chock her; it seems Flora's has near stopped breathing of effect, so she needs more air. Abdullahi smirks from pleasure—saying:—God created Mankind Women to satisfy the Men! That's a woman's purpose and importance! Pardon my French! We're feeling likely to start on the main deal, now, can we?—

Meantime, on ship's upper deck—from nowhere those invaders already—have drawn near the ship, where Flora been there—through all corners of the sea. Where all on board is hearing piercing bangs, combined with weaponry. Follows through a dicey blast that is heard.

Those invaders are paddled in closeness towards the ship. Then they're spinning round on their motorboats; see the attackers have passed through near of a booming ricochet.

... Once those invaders are swum within reach of the ship. Those invaders by now are begun climbing set of steps up, which's having matched to trapezes.

This time reverberates—shaky, in close proximity; which is on high capacity. A man in charge of attackers is of a Northern African look that brings to a halt spar. A Blast is heard! Firearms are shooting. Earshot disrupt with bangs, which has made a giant capacity of a boom, and been causing chaos on this ship.

Meantime, in Flora's cubicle: echo of explosion have felt—so it's been shaky there. Abdullahi, who's by now has stopped his pretence to have Flora, by hearing turbulence—became disturbed; even he is worried:—What the hell is going on up there?—He turns aside with a stare towards exit—gets up; tucks his clothing in, tags on; in that case he positions his gun. In the vein of him being ready shooting any, who would dare enter? Next see Abdullahi is rushed through way in, as leaving her cabin.

Soon after Abdullahi has left—Flora's ears put towards the door seal, and she is listening with breathe caught, while it's frequently in and out ...

She is warily climbed on upper deck; where awful view of those invaders, who are drawn near ship—having emerged from the sea. See they traveled on rubber boats, through remote of smog. Meantime Flora stations on upper deck. Saw the attackers who have occupied the craft; now are firing through a storm of bullets towards . . . A bullet is fired by an attacker— goes flying . . . She forthwith jumps aside; and down; as Flora bends, and hides head within her palms.

The attackers climbing staircases—are passing through; and yet ascend on upper deck. It does be heard odd sharp midway off an open-sea through shaky bangs, this is made Flora—scared stiff in the twinkling of an eye.

Interim Jean-Luc murmurs to her, while looks round:—What has ensued? Invaders have surrounded our ship all through the sea. They loom on high-speed boats. Now it looks as if rescue us all here, is impossible?-

Despite of hostility Flora makes an effort to find out, what effects have; as her face gazed of panicky, asks:—I want ask what has caused chaos.-

One of invaders is togged up in usual; and emergencies having covered themselves with shoals, atop are wearing camouflage in order to shield partly their faces. They are carrying arms along, which contained by spare ammos.

Without warning the muggers are begun shooting straight towards this vessel—from both left and right sites . . .

Sees Flora talks in fear:—There's no a chance to escape? I'm trapped and scared! With nor places to hide, I is only jumping in the sea? Invaders have turned our ship into a state of chaos!—

As she comes across all on board, who are running back or forth on upper deck base, after clashes be taken place. Here spot buildups of those attackers; who are now having taken over control; and given orders on the ship—dire.

Leading them is Sid that in a commanding voice:—Stop ship's steam engine! Next is needed to change en route, as we are set off through the Ocean course . . .—

Subsequent to basically one apiece have become trapped, while hearing—as those attackers are ruled every one.

Sid in English with dominion:—Listen, people! Now you're become hostages! Bear in mind that you're obliged to take refuge on upper deck! Now, all go and sit down!—Those hostages are seated on deck's bottom; with Flora being counted has emerged, stuck between them.

Meanwhile she whispers to Jean-Luc:—My instinct tells of danger with bloodcurdling! Most of times that would lie ahead!—Facing hostility she figures out of caution that, come from the invaders. So far Flora seeks dead set against attackers; and she needs viewpoint from some of those captives.

Period in between Jean-Luc be strict; whispers to her:—Invaders have started a fight, it's clear they sabotaged to occupy a demit ship? They're not eager to let us go? Their plans in no way are my or all onboard by demanding ransom for us?—She nods her head; mumbles:—You right. I'll tell you more, those sailors now—have become truly opposed towards invaders?—Jean-Luc takes breaths; and he is adding:—Except for Abdullahi? Only God knows what he has in mind? I think he is a Psycho?—

Later that day Flora does not shift, and remains just, where she has stood yet; on the same point being arrival of attackers. Despite Flora senses danger—is become valiant focused on attackers. So she is asking daringly:—Where is the ship headed for? Why you'd invaded our vessel?—But those attackers neither are eager, nor they having made an effort to clarify for her. Those captives with Flora counts are seized by invaders, and having placed them on deck. The attackers called themselves— Pirates. One amid them looks angry, cause of madcap; and so he is in a commanding voice has ordered Flora:—Hey woman! Move down to a cubicle, it's for your own safety!—

Flora is become accustomed to her cubicle.

As night arrival her state of health has turned deprives: she looks pale, somewhat being bothering her:—What's happening with me? I feel blunt headache within internal by Razor-sharp sore, cause be aside?—After her back pain began, if lately in flipsides ongoing with a sense of warmth too gluts in her stomach, and lower. As she moves in lavatory alert of odd Flora's mind-set examines hers. She is spotting blood pouring through stream and gashing all the way down. So, she is bleeding internally and profusely. Flora is panicky:—Lord! What's wrong with me? Pain is hot and bothered, within her tight spots, aching. I'm bleeding, thus effect's abnormal? I could bet it has caused off my past ordeals?—

The next morning after carefully assuming on earlier clash, Flora has made a mute decision:—Despite it awful importance I feel be at threat. I won't ask those rivals questions on impulse?—

After a while Flora is climbing on ship's upper deck, she glanced one amid those invaders came into view being in he's late thirties or early forties. He is by a typical Northern-African look this same of a kind, as Abdullahi. With an apt look it has made him a superior above others sailors there. Flora is frantic, but boldly approached him and has raised issue in English:—Please excuse me, sir, I wish to ask for relieve! I fear for my health! The problem is . . . ,—Stops; Flora is short of breathe; so she takes a gulp of air, and she continual:—Sir I feel unwell, if it's possible to hurry up? I urgently need to be taken on shores for treatment in Hospital!—Sid stops her, as is bemused:—Well, darling! Listen, why would I want do a good gesture for you? You seem now in double trouble. And I'm disappointed in you. Did you hear me?—she seems is feeling alarmed, but in poor health. Next sees Abdullahi approached this invader, and they're two having a chat in their traditional language. But Flora is unable to understand; except for a single word be said:-'Medical'. Thus she interrupts them, is edgy:—No sir. Why would you say it?—This pirate looks is enraged, when is alleged to her:—I have been told that you be with Medical? Or I'm wrong?—Flora appears be shocked:—It's true! I have studied Medicine. Who are you people?—But she's stopped by anew comer. This pirate looks of the same kind in her eyes; utters him being firm. Then Sid curiously:—What we're doing here, does not concern you! First of all! Secondly, if you ask questions, woman you'll be, in big troubles . . .—

CHAPTER 19

A few mornings later Flora wakes up in cubicle—but she still has remained indoors.

. . . In a while Flora is hearing that one running pass by her cabin door. Yaks have started among pirates that attended to possibly of a tongue of Bantu or the Lingua Franca.

As Flora looks in illuminator—sad from those memories, thus she talks back to her:—Only two days past since I had seen a dim image of Archipelago throughout those Islands far-off the shores . . .—

Her last hope fades away—she realizes that became edgy:— Liberty is impossible now . . . ?—

At the same day Flora is on ship's deck, where she peek those attackers; her attention has drawn by warning. She spots one of Pirates, who name is—Sid Jakayala. He appears is strongly built, ambitious; a corrupt man that, being cruel at times. Sid is talented, being a fearless conquers; likes to have power over frail one; and awfully wants to possess wealth. He is well-read; and was Scholar in the Western country.

Intervening time Sid talks in English on cell phone:—I tell you clearly what our demands are! We have taken over the ship with hostages aboard! Here are at least three of your people! So that I am warning you're . . .—, He stops; looks around. Sid then speaks into the phone, be edgy:—If your nations refuse to pay for the hostages? Cause they're all held captive here! And being in our custody!—Know how these gangs of invaders' are called themselves Pirates. A pirate is off his wits, and Flora listens carefully to self's voice on other side of a line. He certainly argues with him. Sid then is reacting irately, with a discussing over a cell phone; when has declared:—You've heard me, right?—As someone on the phone line has responded. Sid is reacted:—That's my last warning! If you're nations don't pay ransom for those heads up here? You will find their bodies on the seabed ground!-

Hearing awful exchange of argue, Flora is grown panicky; foremost on her wits of snooping. Sid by now is too staring towards her.

. . . Sid has ended phone call; thus Flora takes a chance on the occasion. She is edgy, walking to him intrusive, and daring started a chat:—Who are you? And what all in your team is doing on the ship?—Sid smirks, then is getting slowly off sit; as he puts left hand in his pocket. He points out by his head; sees his eyes are focused on Abdullahi. Sid then is avowed, sneers, and tackles her, through intense eyes:—Some are called us buccaneers. We are known as Somalia Pirates!—Then Sid looks at her; and says-so is confident:—I trust it's clear to you, who we are? And you're dealing with? Why we are here? What about our tactics, and us to do next?—He stops; and is looking with a smirk into her eyes. Given she ducks her head down awkwardly. Sid hasn't completed his speech; for all he tells her in terms of contradiction:—You're ignorant of the situation? Aren't you, Fleur? You have nor idea who we are?—Flora looks be lost; but edgy:—No, I don't! Maybe I'm naïve! Why you've being nasty to all of us?—Flora is stopped by Sid, who's leader of Pirates. He is irritated:—You ask too much! You're and all aboard will remain hostages, here! Now, and further! He stops. And in a harsh voice pirate preaches more:—Lastly Fleur, truth is if you're Government refusing to pay for your sole, and for these whites too on board? Or trick us at this time . . . Am I right? This is your name?—Flora opts; and bows her head down. The Pirate Sid seems is snappy:—Yet I'm fed up with talking! Get the hell her away from my eyes! Get the woman out!—Flora stops him. She starts alone handle this 'Orator', when yells anxiously:—You don't have the rights! This is a criminal injustice! I demand to return on shores, and be free, to find the Embassy . . .—, But she is prevented this time by Abdullahi, who smirks—meant. He says with scorn:—Shut up, woman! Felling slightly better? A runaway paranoia? Pity, dear!—Abdullahi spins; is facing a stand of the new unruly.—

Abdullahi says-so; be edgy:—Put her back, where she was being held before!—Instead he alone tells promptly to he's P.A. In their natural lingo. Flora looks be tense:—Sir its important if-, Leader of these pirates twist to face Flora; as she stops. It puts across his demand; and Sid points a finger up to her, is annoyed:—And you! I don't want neither see nor hear from you ever! If not say goodbye forever!—

Flora be ushered by a few oddly looking P.A., who are pushing her towards back of stairway. Flora does stay seal; but is taken aback, and simply guessing if one of pirates jumps in and grabs her hand-off; Flora resists . . . Then P.A. seizes her hair with a help from his cohort; and they're both begun dragging Flora downstairs towards cubical. The P.A. Have been discharged from duty; and they proxy being watch-guards—ushered her downstairs.

Approaching Flora's cubicle one of these watch dogs' is thrown her through entryway—right indoor her cubical.

Flora has remained down inner for a few days. Instead she is unable climbing on upper deck without prior warning. But she is daring, when goes up ahead risking; and being wandering round on the upper deck on her free will. Flora mumbles to herself:—I have been kept in dark. If Sid has made new calls? If pirates demand cash for me with eight more folks. All of our fates would-be became a mystery? Cause we're all targets here!—

Given that next Pirates are talking in foreign of deck . . .

While Flora dares into talk to one of those captives.

Jean-Luc whispers to Flora:—Pirates have made plans for all of us captives to be Flora murmurs—be fretful as turns round:—What are pirates' plans? Did you find out anything, Jean-Luc?—He bobs his head, murmurs:—Rumors has that, pirates have concealed as forbidden ship off captives entry. You and I are too counted Flora! What we find if they have loomed yoked us? I keep a low profile, and so should you? I'll keep you posted, Flora . . .

So that info has alarmed her and the rest of hostages.

Meantime on ship's upper deck effect yet got its toll.

So it outcome to be alarmed; those captives emergence in ill health and Flora between are weak collapsed.

Rumors has it that all hostages with Flora counts are having fallen sick; caused of thus deprived conditions . . .

Jean-Luc murmurs; be watchful:—We would get proviso by portion of bread with rations of water?—Flora nods her head; is warily:-I think alike. All us captives want anything to chow. God demit we're half-starved inhere?—

Apart from bad situation has become worsen; surround by deep-sea as the ship cross through heavy storm; follows.

At dusk, in her cubicle Flora is talking to Jean-Luc:—Flora, how you're coping with condition? Flora is edgy, constantly come across murmuring:—In such wild climate our states of health get worse by seasickness. At the last few days, I can hardly walk it feels as if I would lapse. My head is spinning round; which's caused by storms in the ocean; and ship's rotation. This has made situation for us even worse?—

One evening in the ship's cubicle Flora's ears put to the door. Flora hears arguments between those two are serving as P.A. to Pirates on this vessel. Where those two are situated behind door, and one pirate talks in French:—Do you know whereabouts the ship, tactics off crossing to?—Pirate first talks in French:—See our strategy for ship crossing, is to pass through Canal! Then we'll be crossing into Indian Ocean deep waters.—Stop. The first pirate takes breath; and he continual by telling behind door:—Next by map we're heading for the Equator. Since ship's course is towards.

CHAPTER 20

At dawn is hearing of guns with crossfire in all over the vessel, and on deck; origin of propellers flying via, and crashing blares . . .

Sudden a mass Boom! Explosion! And anew explosion! Boom! Then through audible range storm of bullets. So far in cubicle Flora's being scared stiff of that awful view; and she spins; stares via illuminator, where remote to be fogy. Above by odd vast outward shows escorted through helicopters are airborne having smashed with gun firing in that part and outwardly ingot of the air; a warship enclosed this vessel.

Flora's worry is in cubicle, confirmed:—What the heck is going on up there? Battle is in the mid-air! There's no escape? If it becomes unsafe the only way for me is jumping in sea?— Then second explosion! Blast! In Flora's cubical it doesn't feel stable; and base is floating. It seems is become unsafe; so Flora's guesses of the effect. Thus she thinks, be certain:—Cause it could not be worse than were held captive by Pirates?—

Afterward Flora's ear put to the door. She then carefully opens the admission door; looks in peek-hole round via an access.

In stages Flora climbs stairways—glance up round; what is emerged, then she bravely comes on upper deck. As she mounts on deck freezes stiff; what's emergence there: all but pirates are running back and forth. Mood amid that crew have converted into state of a chaos. From all corners of the sea a craft is encircled by jumbo warships—full of ammos. Provisional a pilot helicopter flying; as comes through shower of bullets, bombarding from above advances and straight on target. A mini-device detonates by a remote control—made an explosion! Bang, which has resulted of the ship—is begun shaking.

Flora ran back to cubicle: chaos stood aside; endanger, panicky; yet in close proximity to stairways. A blast! One pirate is into counter attack fired; spotting it goes flying whoosh! A Flora jumps aside; and down by a twist. She scrutiny for bullet that is flying out indirectly over through; and hits; has wounded one Pirate . . .

Meantime on ship's upper deck—aerial . . . A battle is out of control. Forces have attacked, and now destroyed some of equips; aimed to catch pirates, who have destabilized that crew, and for safety reasons are aimed freeing those hostages and others.

. . . Safely clinging to cable cord that task force is slowly on. Prime targets seen by the Forces are having bungee jumps; and landing down on upper deck, through zigzag out . . . These forces are jumping:—Frrrr!—View they are equipped with machine guns and ammos. Lieutenant in a command voice:— Let's go find them, guys! Go-move it!-

Later stuck between stairways—machinery zone sees that task force with Lieutenant in command is dropping down through stairs; entering ship's duct. The light is on low beam dim; obscured; sees incoming rear half-arm-length group of navies are on foot. Kruger is beside Sgt. Balthazar in front with a torch; as are listening warily for footsteps. Given that force ahead, and down through approach. The forces are hearing echo as one; reached for guns, which's concealed under their waistbands; and they pulling out in tandem with those advanced footsteps . . .

Meanwhile, out in the engine room—inward of Machinery section a self hustles. Here sees that group holding bags with odd objects; and ahead wooden boxes be opened prior. On verge one enters; this is Sid Jakayala—leader of Pirates. Sid joints a grouping; and is working equally as others, says-so:— I'll smash audio by side of a spare one! Then I would pack them, and fold boxes are up here.

Next emerged Abdullahi; is moving out heavy stuff there to matching side off the entry—tick for tack. Seen he is covering that undamaged stuff over with tarpaulin.

While on upper deck the armed forces have found Pirates.

Given that squad is ensued to bear; which have packed with gears up. That unit with Lieutenant is entering engine Cabin; then drawling fast through; and being inserting their blob pirates' with chuckles. That force is tamping hectic into audibly, with dull click . . . Then another click; and guns in the hands off Pirates are getting cleared by that navy force. One amid these forces takes in hand; known him be in charge of that operation.

Lieutenant shout in command voice:—Freeze! Turn around all of you! Or I'll order to shoot . . .—

Amid activity pirates have stopped, without more ado; hearing that one of those squawks being panicky. A first pirate:—Don't shoot us! We beg you!—Sergeant looks be annoyed:—Drop your weapons Pirates, my Ass!—Sergeant then turns to face this strange man, certainly a leader; by instant asking him:—What we've to do with pirates? After that, Lieutenant?—He' is at a halt. Lieutenant is tackling the Pirates handily in a command voice:—You're Pirates assholes! My unit and I've got trigger meant at all of you're bloody brains! Hey you are, there! What's your name?—Sid says in part English:—No, Anglais! I don't speak English!—To which Lieutenant being annoyed:—Fuck you all . . . !—

Here appears pirate, whose spoke French spins; has shown his face in coming into the light being Sid Jakyala that opt a fast runs off Engine sector, without task force being able find out of this bandit's true identity . . .

Meantime Flora stayed in her cabin—is scared. Caused by her health being off agony; she's feeling back-pain—at the brink of collapsing every minute. As a result Flora lies down on top of bed-cover.

. . . Sudden the door gets widely open; where at the front of be covered entrance has emerged Abdullahi . . .

Pro tem, out way in those navies are walked in step-by-step—all as one carrying arms under camouflages—still have concealed their weapons. That force is moved forth through an aisle as to find pirates; who have hidden somewhere in vessel. Given one of that navy is gushing audibly into walkie-talkie. Next Lieutenant takes over from him, says via two-way radio:—There we were under going to be five Pirates at least wait for us in fill with ammos on hand!—The first navy demand:—We have a bunch to deal with process, is that right, Lieutenant?—Commander's voice on walkie-talkie:—How close you're, second-in-command?—Says Lieutenant into two-way radio:—My bunch of navy is kept close to each-other. But the ship's shitty; it's not a big one. We are sited within hundred nautical miles of thirty degrees south as twenty seven minutes—off North-West. Cause the ship is stuck between inland waterways, far-off the shore!—Commander's voice on two-way Radio is heard:—Just put adequate volts into Pirates, they'll talk within half an hour!—

. . . In a flash on upper deck someone began offensive attack; thus far the effect has been felt within the access way.

Lieutenant is away of Radio; worried:—Hush . . . all, lay down!—The Lieutenant allegedly reminisces to verify; tells, be jumpy voice on Radio:—Nice try, Commander! You've nearly blown us up! Did you want to kill us? I'd make shit my pants from panic! Sorry Commander, for being rude . . .—, Commander's voice on radio:—Okay! See on the situation as to deal with! Take care of your guys and of those Hostages! Don't get your guys under fire and in risk to fight! Lieutenant, I won't keep you longer, to-do! Take care!—He talks via the walkie-talkie:—Yes, Command in chief! I'll be in touch, pronto!—Kruger looks gloomy. As he spins attending to one of those forces. And this time Lieutenant is addressing Sergeant, Balthazar:—Yep, chief was right! I need that position on the God demit shooting of guns! Where's from?—Sergeant takes action:—Let's go and check all demit cabins, then . . .—

In cubicle Flora sees Abdullahi enter it; and jumps up is on foot. She doesn't stand a chance to escape. At spot he is running ahead of Flora; and he gets her hands by tough seizes. Abdullahi grabs her hair; then puts a grenade in Flora's hand. She senses grenade can explode any minute; so is scared and being breathless. Thus Flora is in taken gulps of air; and tried be calm with her own aim as to stay out of danger. She is cautious of grenade; with her own mind-set of plot; that capsizes it back to him. He wits her aim to divert and tackles backwards; and inserts from his waistband a gun. Given that Abdullahi is obsessed with her; and so he outsmarts her:—Don't even think about! You will go up with per head on the ship. We all will be blow up finally!—She is grinding her teeth:—You're bloody killer! Give up? You're not the only one on ship! Here other peoples, me amongst, are not ready to die? Go jump in the sea the world will be a better place off you!—He yells is hostile:—Shut the fu** up! Bitch!-

Meantime, out in the ship ails—the Lieutenant is giving orders to that force being watchful. A Lieutenant hums, as signs by hands:—Guys, carry on checking all remain cabins on this ship! We need back up plan to catch this person, whose given orders to bloody Pirates?—Next a bomb explodes remote on the deck blast! This has resulted off hard-hitting these navies; seeing them lie on bottom; still are acting in defense. These forces are hanging on to, which lead to a powerful bang; and having become a cover up for the insurgents by their resistance . . .

Step by step the forces with Lieutenant between head up—are looking at each other. Kruger is genuinely concern for their security he bends down; is worried:—Are you all okay there, Sergeant?—Sergeant raises, and nods with his head:—Yep, Lieutenant, we all OK!—Lieutenant turns round and whispers:—Come on you dudes let's get up! Now I'll cover you're backs. We need to check, if bloody Pirates killed our guys? Sergeant is positive:—Yes, Lieutenant in chief!—Kruger murmurs, signs by hands:- Sergeant, stop! We'll be shifting in pairs, as a convoy. So, pirates won't be able firing on us! Okay?—

Not long after Flora in the cubicle has kept froze; thus event gambling with her life, it also is made her defenseless—resisting Abdullahi. A sudden door gets wide open; on verge are having emerged those two navies . . .

Meantime out—in ship ails Lieutenant with navies are approached cabin; door be locked. The forces looking at each-other are in touch through gestures by Lieutenant mostly intended to check these cubicles. Then one of the forces has glued plastic bomb aim to launch. Blast! Boom! It has come from outer walls off compartment, and make a collision. Sees knocks down a few armed forces. Rips off the door off it hinges. Light goes off. Peers the door—swings back and forth.

Sergeant Balthazar is toward inner, when stumbled through a hook that, narrowly hanged of door way—into cubicle. "Oops! Ouch!"—On a whim a stool is flown directly; have knocked off their feet; seeing first falls down—is Sergeant. A Lieutenant shouts worriedly:—Go down, guys!—He alongside those other two navies; who are from outcome—having angled down.

There comes into the light a man of Northern African look. That navy unit is glanced; and recognized him from earlier confrontation; since the man is—Sid Jakayala.

CHAPTER 21

Shortly Flora stands beside Abdullahi, is hearing one re-opens cabin door; where are lastly emerged the navies having wore a dark tint uniforms their heads are covered with helmet; camouflage wore on top for their safety. Those navies are fully equipped through ammos; then they're started loading machine-guns.

Those two navy stances are intense; not without hope for Flora's safe release. She is ahead scared; and stops them involving a warning:—Don't come close! He has a gun! He forced me too hold grenade. You be careful, cause we all here could die!-

Sudden those navies have spotted a bomb device, by which Flora is danger—the main target. Abdullahi rejoice be cynical:—Oh, yeah policemen! It is nor a joke here! She really covers a grenade in her hand!-, these last words he has uttered with irony. Pulling up his gun to her neck; Abdullahi with hilarity is in a biting wit:—If I shoot her it's going to blast the whole ship with all of you that must die . . .—Periodic is a navy in angry reply, who points hand at Flora. The first navy tries to make him:—Hey, your! Let the woman go!—Abdullahi in his place smirks; is ironic:—Baa! I like risk destroyed by guilt!—He stops as is heated:—Pity, asshole! Threaten us with a grenade? We know well than you what a bomb is! Let her go! We can try replace with combating. It's fairly inconvenience to rip off a bloody shell! Let's fight?—Flora stops him; says intently:—He's name is Abdullahi. And he's allied with Pirates!—Stop. She is breathing deep; and graves a fast talk by plead and with anxiety:—Officer I feel sick! Cause I urgently must be examined by Doctors!—She turns to face Abdullahi; and tackles him; senses back up by the navies. Then Flora began blaring to him:—Abdullahi, don't you get it?—Though he ignores her; in his place turns to a navy one is addressing him:—I'm eccentric, and a businessman! Here are my citizens poor! But I would like to make a deal with you're, if not then . . .—

Next one of those navies stops him; involves quirk of fate. The first navy is daringly:—If not, than what? You will blow all us up then? Is that it, Abdullahi?—One of those navies has made a slipshod move. Then Abdullahi is backward; and begun fooling around; see he is shaking Flora's hand firmly. Abdullahi ahead pulls down a gun; by which's meaning too act of violence towards all. He is angry; as his hand shaky:—One more move, and she goes off! Gain you all too with hers! Hold on that crazy ass of yours, bloody Police!—A first navy smirks; but be tense:—You know something; firstly, we aren't Police! We're the Special Forces. You're Dodo if think? Give it up you, Son of Bitch!—Abdullahi is fussy:—Don't you realize? Can't you see she's a beauty? I have not got a chance to make her mine! One's life become empty, coz we're fancy for finest stuff, but can't get? Looks at Flora:—I paid for her! I own the woman! And can doom, whatever I'd like . . .—, He becomes distracted by a navy one that meant of vulgar. In that case first navy is on edge—yelling:—Listen, you asshole! She is not your assets! She's a human! And if you're inapt to let her go?—This first navy turns his head round; next asks delicate her:—What's your name, dear?—Flora looks be desperate:—I'm Fleur, but not from Africa . . .—, The first navy stops her, spins back, and shouting be edgy Abdullahi:—Hey, your! Who thou fu**, do you think, you're? If you're really thinking we going to be scared and react to your fu***** fanatical bullshit? Give to me this grenade!—Abdullahi in its place is ironic:—What if I don't? What if I feel like to blow her, and the ship up?—Smirk; he still is fixed with grasp of her hand into a grenade; ad shifting a hand from her hair, then stoops to her collar. Flora is shy, as emerged stone-white of fear, with wide-open eyes; given her free hand trembles that she tries to hang on. A first navy says-so be firm:—I repeat you're a crazy with all your pirates and fucking P.A.! Let the woman go! I warn you for the last time! Do you hear me?—Abdullahi is acting by contradiction in terms:—A solid façade! Boom!—He shows both of his hands up in the air, where clutch a grenade; smirks in irony. The navy one stops him; of regret:—Listen, you! Cut that shit! Let her go! Let's make a deal? You've got your ship! What else do you want?—A first navy takes deep breaths, and prolongs to tell:—You're dead set against the Law such as: arms race, possession of drugs! Ride out; go, where you've planned! Why you need her with those hostages?—Then a first navy stops. He is with a critical eye to him. As the second navy in a sweet talks:—Abdullahi, why don't you give the grenade to me? Let's make a deal? This fuss must to end now! You can't kill the woman?—

A sudden amends: the second navy is thrown an army made knife it flown straight and gets into Abdullahi's upper arm that fleshy tissue injuring him:—"Ouch!"—

In ship's ails Lieutenant alongside with other two navy officers are entered cubicle; they're have glimpsed Sid been there. The Sergeant is annoyed:—Hysterical? Pity you're asshole!—Sid wouldn't give up easily. He then unexpectedly attacks Sergeant with a pipe; by knocking this last out. Given that Sergeant Balthazar collapses down into the flooring. Lieutenant is heated:—What a fu****** mess inhere is?—He then spins as a result of running after Sid that is made an attempt to escape—passing through the access. Lieutenant shields Sergeant with these rests of navies from a gunshot; as Balthazar reloads his gun in mid-run . . .

. . . Sid in cubicle stumbles through entry that is hanging off its hinges at the heart of the cubicle. Spotting the injured Sergeant goes down . . . When Lieutenant jumps into combating through clash with Sid. He picks a desk and heaves is dazed at Lieutenant, who goes down and angles.

. . . Kruger is throwing punches at Sid over but messes up. Sid swings over. Smack! Bang! Sudden a single blow over Kruger's stomach Sid is with a metal pipe in his hand; it does hurt Lieutenant that spotting—he is unmoved . . .

To shield Kruger from Sid's pipe wielding, Sergeant lunges towards pair's off to get between exchanges of their blows. Sid is just managed hard to smack Sergeant by a metal pipe. Impact of blows floors Sergeant. Seeing as Sid goes for the kill . . .

Only he is stopped in his tracks, by Lieutenant Kruger that growls:—Arrrgghhh! You're asshole!—Then Sid yells in French:—Mer-de!—The Lieutenant shifts aim; and punches blow with whips pipe of Sid's hand! Sid pulls a gun out of waistband; and tries to shoot at him. Sees Jakayala is ahead of Sergeant. With a smirk Sid starts to run away. Kruger is after him with anew attempt to fire through a tube, and using it as a shield. A bullet knocks Sid into he's leg tissue. Sid goes down; but still has it eerie leer upon his face. Lieutenant is standing above Sid angry:—Drop your gun, asshole! I'm more than ever, in a shitty mood! Especially after you're Pirates having set a trap for my guys!—Then the Lieutenant spins to face Balthazar is worried:—Are you okay, Sergeant?—He tries to get up:—Yes, chief! The Bastard wouldn't take me that easy!—See Kruger bend down to grab him:—Come on Sergeant, get up! Slowly.—Then he spins—facing those rest of navies, and focus on them:—Now guys you'll guard us. Let's go—we need to find those hostages?—

Later that force under Lieutenant's command, is in ship's ails having approached the cabin door next to Sid's compartment. He murmurs—points to a lock:—Dudes, the door is locked up!—Afresh the Lieutenant twists doorknob handles; right on entry; seeing as Kruger is outwardly—unmoved. One navy is attempting to unlock the door; began an assault using the machine gun; with loads of shooting.

The first navy signs with eyes; murmurs:—I'll try blow a god demit door?—Lieutenant's head move up and down with a wink:—Dude has to get a system in your hands!—Sudden blast! A plastic bomb is discharged door whole boom! The Lieutenant tugs cabin's door to open, this is seen come out more of a hinder—it hardly be hanged on its way in . . .

Slow-moving Lieutenant with other navies are entered cabin, where comes into view a group of at least seven. Amid three are emerged white persons. A bunch of that ship's crew is held captured, given all being panicky.

In Flora's cubicle—briefly the few navies have emerged at doorsill. This time Flora is seen among them. Hearing as one of those navies is verifying to the Lieutenant.

This first navy is edgy, signals with eyes towards his partner:—Bustard wouldn't let the woman go!—When the Lieutenant spins towards the navies, is taking in hand opt. In a command voice he:—Dudes, follow me right now. We need to locate the leader of Pirates!—He stops:—And we must find out, which's made those phone calls? Can any of you point them to us?—

In that case Flora lifts her hand up, and without consent says-so be nervy:—I'll help you identify this character Sid, who's given orders to Pirates! He has also made the phones calls, and demanding ransom for all of us here!—

Out in Sid's cabin—sees a Lieutenant in company with a few of those good navies have entered that aimed cubical. Flora is eager; talks fast:—Before ship has belonged to Abdullahi. Yet it's occupied by Sid, who too has stayed there, I'm sure of it!—

A bit later in line Flora enters cabin—saw her beside the Sergeant is loomed over Abdullahi, who's sustained wounds. Due to ordeal a navy is overtaking Abdullahi, who is being detained from Balthazar to handle him?—View—Sergeant puts a set handcuff into Abdullahi's wrists.

Walking in Flora's cubicle spots a few navies one among them is the Lieutenant; sees him being engaged in the line of commune through a walkie-talkie.

Given Flora is listening clued-in there to a man that is with agitation, this is second navy yaks using two-way radio, utters:—All the hostages aboard are alive. One among them is a young woman! She needs Medical help! And we want to take her on shores to a nearest Hospital?—Lieutenant becomes intolerant; be a fast replaces, when takes over from a Navy speaker; he's implying is furious. Lieutenant talks loud via on two-way radio:—Yep, commander they are all shit-sick here! What's more? Here's a new prototype between Pirates this one doesn't speak English. So we need a translator now, as to . . .—, at the same sec. Flora stops him. Then in protest Flora says-so of fret and loud:—Bastard! Hopeless liar! He knows English demit well! Above all Sid is leader of those Pirates!—Sid stops her—says in anger:—Shut the fu** up! Yes, you Bitch!—He made a shift toward Flora's site and grabs her wrist firm. A sudden jump in, by Jean-Luc, who attempts to guard Flora. Impulsive jump too by Lieutenant in to free Flora's hand; he then puts the two-way radio aside. But Jean-Luc speaks first. He seems is sympathizing Flora; when peeks at her; he then alleged. Jean-Luc angrily says:—Leave her alone! You're Jerk!—Abdullahi is held his hands up in the air. Jean-Luc in he's early thirties, medium-to-tall with his height. He is well spoken English, still has a minor French accent. Though he is an okay looking chap; brunet-colored; sea-blue-eyed; with slight tan by affect of sun ray. He comes into view by unique character, even if be unshaven; among principle of a man's with appear that suits his features.

Whereas Lieutenant that is prying:—Yeah, leave woman to be! Well done, man! What's your name? He reacts:—I'm Jean-Luc, and working for 'Medicine sans Frontiers'! I'm in support to treat those Africans, who are being in poor health. I was also held captive by Somali Pirate on this ship!—After Abdullahi has got handcuffed, without ado speaks up, he has dull eyes; is pessimistic:—Well, well it's the end of the line. This day has become regret for existing to all of us aboard!—Then Lieutenant turns round to see him:—Why so you're pessimistic? Cause you could not cash in for whites on this ship?—So he is genuine cautious, else Abdullahi is given the impression of being dull, but he is unmoving pro in his eyes . . .

A sudden Jakayala has interrupted; when exchanged from Abdullahi, Sid has dull eyes, he begun in a sharp is implying:— You know something officers, Sudanese have a wise say . . .—, he's breathing deeper:-" . . . Salt comes from—the North! Gold comes from—the South! Water comes from—the Sea! Cause Money come from—the Whites!"—A prone reflection in the task force's eyes that are spotting by means with harsh abhorrence towards Pirates. Lieutenant smirks; in quirk of fate says:—Well, surprise-surprise! You do speak English, don't you, Sid? Hey, that is not the end for you here, and you're P.A. Soon all of you'll wish that you never born! Sid be assured:—Don't be so cocky, chief! I know my rights!—Kruger is annoyed:—What the Hell you'll do, dickhead!—He disrupts him; alleged is heated, turns to Balthazar. But Lieutenant commands:—Sergeant take the Hell away Pirates on shores! Pronto!-

Later Lieutenant Kruger is half-whispering being cunning and so his voice as he smirks to Sergeant Balthazar:—You know Sergeant, the woman, Flora's absolutely stunning! On one thing Abdullahi was right about . . .—But the Lieutenant is disrupted by Sergeant that says-so be serious:—Listen Lieutenant, I'll tell you as man-to-man:—Piss off! Not long ago you've got married, back home . . .—

University building

PART—VI

Surprising—Live Out

CHAPTER 22

Arrival jointly at twilight on shore's Hospital, by which have hostage earlier drama held by the pirates on ship earlier. Here are detainees desperately but patiently waiting in a queue for their check ups.

. . . Flora's being apt liberated for the first time; along with those other eight hostages are counted.

It's become visible that her state of health be poor. Due to side effects Flora is taken into the clinic, ahead of those seven other sick detainees. She goes for a check-up to the Doctor's office; in that case . . .

Proceeding by the medical check in a hospital ward Flora observes Doctor is calling upon that nursing staffs.

A few minutes later: Flora wouldn't let go of Jean-Luc's hand. He then instructs Medical staffs that are begun running back and forth. Of an affect she is urgently given injection;

and into narcosis. She is disturbed; by now feels weak, looks as if she has not quite admitted been present; thus she made inquiry. Flora is restless:—Doctor what's going on? Is there something wrong with me? The second surgeon in brogue English, affirmed her:—Forth major, dear! Don't worry we can fix you well! You will be fit again!—Surprisingly Jean-Luc emerges there, and refers to a Doctor. Jean-Luc seems be uneasy:—I'm a doctor! If you let me join you're in surgical procedure? May I be at hand in the operating Theater?—The first surgeon gazes at his ID:—Who are you? How did you get that? Where's you're from? He is solid, tells loudly:—As I said before I'm a Doctor! It's be approved by the Hospital Boards for me to do this surgery!—The two doctors and nurses are staring at a stranger with doubt; while shaking with their limbs. Then one among them bobs his head is in agreement—the second surgeon nodded, has declared:—Okay! Let's go! Join us, no time!—The man—second surgeon turns around; then talks to that medical staff:—All get ready for the surgery!—

. . . Doctor alongside those nurses are placed Flora from bed into a trolley; has circled round her; and attends to medic staff. The second surgeon:—Is all prepared for Operation?—A nurse mutely Nods her head. A Doctor then bends over to Flora. The doctor informs a nurse about. The second surgeon made known:—Take this patient to the operating theatre, promptly!—

After approaching operating theatre—Flora yet senses drowsiness: heavy-eyed be closed, her brain increasingly disconnected—in that case being essence of her falling down. That excel of illumination is faded away off; as her vision be blurry. Flora has passed out into, and is losing consciousness.

CHAPTER 23

In New Haven, Flora's hometown meantime outside is seen snow.

View it is the closing stages of winter. Here is a rainy day in the New Haven—plenty of snow.

On the porch of a visitor, who's being buzzing into the front Door that happen to be Whitmore's residence—bell rings in Hear resonance amplified of one's footsteps.

Within the house: Flora's mother Virginia is on foot and approaching the front door. There on the porch sees the same man, whom they had a conversation with a while ago.

A caller:—Mrs Whitmore, good Afternoon! Is your husband home now?—Virginia by a confused look:—Yes, he is. What can we do for you? Have you got any news related to our daughter, Flora? Is she Okay?—The visitor: respond—Yes! And that's why I specially come to your home: to talk to both of you! May I come in?—She steps aside:—Oh, yes, of course! Please come inside, Mister Manson!-

See the visitor is strolling ahead followed by Virginia at length behind, as they walk in the living room. Here appears are sitting Flora's grandma Mrs. Kathryn, and beside her husband Hamish. Count in too Flora's father with her brother Jason that is watching with interest the news programme on TV screen.

When this visitor with Virginia behind emerges in their living room. She brings to everyone's attention, talking loud and fret:—Jason, switch off that bloody TV!—Jason in that case spins around; there he is facing a visitor, whose appears. He then spanks his dad; Karl means with irritation, by his turning round:—What the Hell do . . .—,He then stops once facing this caller, who astonishes him:—My apology sir! You see, we both have been watching the late news! And I found that in Africa Pirates had taken over a ship with hostages aboard . . .—,

Then the caller cuts short him—is involved summarily of an issue:—That's exactly why I came here to tell the whole family! I only want all of you not to get worried . . .—, Virginia grows to be frantic when disturbs him, her face has changed fast:—What news have you brought us?—The visitor:—Don't be alarmed. On one thing you right, sir, when I came you in watched the

News. The ship that taken over by Pirates with hostage aboard off Somalia. Unlucky your daughter was a hostage there. The navies among others found her. We received a call from the Embassy a short time ago about her, and so I rushed to inform you're . . .—,He is interrupted by Karl, who is rising up, but looks upset:—What were saying—my Flora was held captured by Pirates? How she got there in the first place? She's married for God sake, Mbeki?—Karl is said. This visitor let the family know:—Apparently she is not. In compliant with Tanzanian Law—marriage outside their country is unlawful and not be accepted there. Genuinely Flora's health is Okay! You must not worry about her . . . !—Virginia appears there being sad; apart to this last seen Mrs. Kathryn is alike; as her husband, Hamish seems be on edge. Next Virginia speaks up her mind is crying with a grave voice:—My poor child! I need to be in the air at once to Africa! I want to see my daughter, and take Care of her!—This visitor:—I'm not aware of the whole story occur. But your daughter right now is placed in hospital. I suggest for all of you to calm down and not to rush in. You won't be able to fly now, on reason that you have to apply for a Visa, which shall take quite a while for processing. I advise you ought to be patient. She will be fine, and is to arrive back home . . .—

CHAPTER 24

The next morning in African hospital within screened-off area see doctors and staffs are having examined patients. Within one of wards is seen Flora—undergoing critical methodical check-ups. See emergency in haste had—after lead-in of her surgery procedure; that she slept around fourteen hours in a row . . .

Sees those gents in a ward two of them are doctors with Jean-Luc count up. A third man is from Flora's homeland Embassy. It's clear as one verifying for her viewpoint at the center of a marquee that be hidden; and yak between those doctors; who wore white robs; with stereoscope resting up and round he's neck have circled. She hears as visitors are whispering . . .

Be awaken Flora feels sharp pain below her stomach, which still is hurting her; since ghastly bleeding had arouse.

Aside from this inapt her upper limbs are feeling stiff; and she finds connected to a drip, it seems Flora is impatient, then her becoming suddenly upset. To her stun that medical staffs are spoken English; she then daringly disrupts those doctors talking. Flora yells in English:—Excuse me please, what's going on here? Why am I having that drip in?—Jean-Luc avoids her from asking:—Don't you remember, Fleur?—The second surgeon, so-called:—Yesterday evening, when you were brought in hospital? You have the undergone operation?—Flora began purposely to evoke—what was her reminiscence of incidents before. Yet those doctors have disturbed her nostalgia. She inhales. All at once she is hearing between visitors are having a discussion. Next they are involving Flora in opposite view; as one of them is looking into her eyes, with a lucid query in English:—Is your name happens be Fleur Whitmore, by any chances?—She looks be shocked:—Yes! So what?—Flora attends to another man, who is emerged being a Doctor; as she asks bluntly, and her voice is shaky:—Doctor! Can you explain, what is wrong with me? Why you've required a preceded surgery on me?—Jean-Luc imposes, professed:—You had a miscarriage, I'm sorry! You're bleeding profusely . . .—, the second doctor stops him; takes a deep breathe; see to it:- . . . It may be arisen for few days? Surgical procedure was necessary for us to carry out, then!—

The first surgeon talks gently:—Still, don't be alarmed you will able to bear kids in the future . . .—, He has been disrupted by Flora, who seen that a new arrival goes via curtains. She is just now become upset. Out of her grief Flora is asking doctor for reason that, resulted of her still being sobbing, as her talk with interval:—Doc, what is your meaning of miscarriage?— The first surgeon gently, tells, sees to:—You were pregnant. I'm sorry!—Flora becomes disturbed, is crying heavily with half intervals in-between. She then began in protest asking:—What was timing of my pregnancy?—The second surgeon:—Well, at least eight weeks. Genuinely it happens by the first pregnancy. You're going to be fine, trust me!—Flora still is distressed:— How can you be so cruel? To ask me that? Demit I'll be OK! Do you realize with cost of my baby's life?—She is crying. It follows that first surgeon calls upon the nurses. In that case he yells anxiously:—Nurse! Come here pronto! Give this patient a shot of a tranquilizer, without hesitation!—

. . . Once receiving an injection Flora is becalms peaceful. Seeing after that she is progressively falling asleep . . .

Later that same evening, when Flora's wakes up in a hospital's ward: awareness of her losing the baby that she was carrying before; made an effect and brings her again to sorrow; with a quiet conclusion to. Flora talks out of grief:— . . .

That's the price I've paid on upheaval of proceeding through flow of bleeding, then on a demit ship? I hadn't even paid heeds . . .—As an unfamiliar person that arises matching to her bed is disrupting her. This one—a middle-age woman, who's getting drawn in; and started chew the fat. She says is straight to the point, in a tender voice:—Hello, Flora! I can see you're awakened? My name is Elizabeth. I work here as a doctor-psychologist . . .—, Flora stops her restive:—I haven't asked for psychologists!—Elizabeth looks in her eyes:—Flora, I do care, what you suffered. You mustn't torture yourself, dear,-Flora says fast; agitatedly:—It is not of your concern! This is my life! With your societal hypocrisy, won't work on me! Okay?—Elizabeth says be delicate:—Flora, please, let me help you! If not you'll be crazy! Flora you're already on a brink of Psychosis you emotionally have . . .—, Flora yet cut short by Elizabeth the Psychologist, is implying fiery:—You telling that I am suffering from psychosis, now?—Elizabeth's respond:— After the ordeal! When you were held captive on the ship. You've might developed it? If you're, Flora, let me heal you? Unless you prefer to be cured by the new Doctor, Flora?—She stops her:—I don't hold anything against you. Unless I would like to be treated by him!—Flora points hands to a doctor: a man; who early was held captive like her; Jean-Luc prior had told her of thus miscarriage . . .—, Elizabeth reacts:—You mean Jean-Luc? If that's your preference, Flora?—Elizabeth turns round is facing Jean-Luc. Flora disrupts her saying:—And, yes, Elisabeth I prefer him!—She ducks her head up and down:—I be acquainted with Jean-Luc well and I trust him!—Elisabeth turns in front Jean-Luc, whom Flora's knew well and being glad to see; after coming to life from surgery. Elizabeth looks with amazement:—Jean-Luc, what do you think? Will you to take care of her? Helping her to overcome complications? Until she makes a full recovery? Oh, before I forget Jean-Luc you may stay in Hospital. Well, if Flora wants that? For her sake I'll try my best.—A Jean-Luc beam is amused.

Flora is in a hospital's ward—under Doctor Jean-Luc's observation, which's developed with her treatment great improvement. He would come—in her ward a lot, after his shift:—Flora, sorry, not yet out of the woods. It means not be allowed you to go outside!—He stops; take gulp of air; he looks at her; then in a calm voice. He then continual:—not only to heal wounds under surface of your skin. To clear of that take care of your emotional scar developed into condition pro you by nervous post-trauma . . .

Flora smiles:—I know and utterly agree with you, Jean-Luc! But after the whole lot that I've gone through . . .—She discontinues; is crying. And again she prolongs, as is distressed:—Since I had met Mbeki . . . So it was being an effect of my journey—to Africa . . .—

Flora's intuition gave a hint for her of having faith in Jean-Luc with reliance.

She would spend hours with Jean-Luc, who's shown up out of the blue. He would get straight into talking with her picturing with his grave face in an enclosed ward. Jean-Luc by a severe tone:—Flora, I'm free today! On a daily basis jobs—all for the health of my patients!—Flora is witty:—So I've heard gossip that proofs you're a fine doctor, and human with good-nature?—He's with a smile reacting:—Well I try my best triumph over beating ill-health . . . I have retained on good terms with those African patients'! Now, Fleur let's talk about your tragedy? Tell me about your crisis, which you have undergone. How you had end up, and held captive, on a God demit ship, and by Pirates?—

In hospital Jean-Luc would often come to see Flora that is resting in screened-off area. The instant he is free from duty, and he would come for rap session with her . . .

Later that day doctor, Jean-Luc would turn up switch to her surprise during he's shifts to have a chat, tells her his story:—Few years ago I had applied to the 'Medicines

San Frontier' to the chief?-

From time to time Doctor, Jean-Luc would update Flora. He is excited:—Doctor's job is sympathizing with ordinary people. And care for patients—try to provide Medical emergency for those, who went through tough lives and them being desperate in needs . . .

Over a week have past. In a hospital ward Flora is appeared being physically much stronger. Despite that she has dropped a size or two of her body-weight . . .

That medical staffs would have taken great care of Flora in the course of her recuperation in hospital. Most of all Flora and Jean-Luc are into affection to each other. That benefits for both—thanks to their friendliness.

Once Jean-Luc arrives as usual to check up on Flora in an obscured ward. It made an affects he is become wordless; Flora looks excited and healthy. She beams at him; and he has noticed that, she is wearing make-up on her face. He sights it that is amazed him. And Jean-Luc exclaims, as he's eyes wide-open:—Flora, you looking radiant? Do you feel better? What's happening, tell me?—Flora is keen to tell:—You won't believe it, if I tell you? Today I'd guest Consul from my homeland, he's promised that, once I released from hospital, I'll be granted a Passport! And return to my country! Isn't it amazing?—Flora pulls her head up; looks up at him; then a stop; asking:—Doc, but you turn pale? What's the matter with you? Aren't you happy for me, Jean-Luc?—He is with a nervous smile:—Of course, I'm happy, silly! I am also proud of myself, with a great result of me be able healing you. And I triumph over beating that demits psychosis!—She spanks his arms. He calms himself down and encouraged—when Jean-Luc comes back with a respond . . .

CHAPTER 25

Another week has passed. Doctor's office, in hospital.
A person is knocking at the door in Doctor's office. As Jean-Luc gets up of his sit and opens the door at the entrance is shown up Flora. He grins, despite is seeing being astonished.

Flora was discharged from Hospital two days ago . . .

Here Jean-Luc with a concern looks, says:—I am surprised seeing you here? Is there something wrong with you Fleur? Are you feeling unwell?—Flora instead beams is excited:—Not at all! I'm feeling very well! I only came here to say my thanks the lot that you've done for me!—She stops—take breaths; and tells:—Doc, I couldn't leave without say goodbye to you myself! I feel to like it! I leave! My flight scheduled for tomorrow, midday. Adieu, Jean-Luc! I do wish you all the best!—Jean-Luc's face alters: the shine disappears from his eyes, as the skin texture turns into pale. He then gets up off his chair and draws near, where she is seated. He with a nervy smile:—Flora, I am glad that you have taken troubles coming here, and saying goodbye?—She says politely:—How can I not? That med staffs and you personally have cared for me a great deal! Doctor you've told me the last time, when we'd chat about working, for which's you've said that Organization being called?—In that case he bobs his head; gently:—Listen, Flora, I finish my shift soon. Can you wait for me? We'll go some place to talk?—Flora talks by joy:—Okay! I'll be glad spend time with you! In fact I've a whole evening to myself. No special plans for tonight!—

Flora appreciated that they're having developed into bond. Given between those two are hooked on a friendship.

Benefit on the doubt Jean-Luc brought her back. View as Flora being almost healthy again, like spiritually as well physically . . .

Flora with a wide smile:- . . . I'm healthy again! It couldn't be possible, if it wasn't for you, Doc!—Given that Flora starts telling him a story of her life . . .—Taken breaths in-between, she is prolonged by telling . . . She is crying. She then takes breaths; composes; and tells him more:—I recall cruelty that set from the start, when my husband sold me . . .—, Area under discussion of those Pirates that claims her being conscious of the situation, back then on a vessel . . . She takes breaths; as prolongs to tell a story:—Next I'd been held captive on the ship with seven more hostages by Pirates! How we'd all be seized? We've got freed, at last from captivity . . .—, Flora turns to face him with a grin. Instead Jean-Luc is raising an issue:—My hint, did you consider starting dating, again?—Flora startled; breathes deep. By more thinking, Flora sees to:—Not for a long shot, Jean-Luc! Despite of odds, I'm glad overcome hardship; I have got through, and now being feeling one of luckiest human alive . . .

Later at night the couple decided going to tavern. This pair spends time past midnight not making love, in they're place discussing; with attention towards. Flora raises an issue:—How on Earth awful as that is possible?—He and tensely is telling his story by a grave look:— . . . I couldn't be heartless to face fatality in the world! So I've decided travel to Africa with the aim of working! And take part to safe human lives! I intend be of medical help just now! Flora is gloomy:—Despite all odds, which those Africans have disrespected me, and treated as an outsider; with cool shoulders, but I do feel concerned for the population!—Jean-Luc interrupts with importance so as to make her stay, and listen:—Let's change the subject? Your flight is for tomorrow, I'm aware of it. Look if you change your mind and stay, Flora? And apply to an Org so we can work jointly to assist those poor and sick Africans?—Flora:—Wow! Whoa? Doc waits a sec.! I'm flying to my homeland! I didn't say that I'm keen to stay in Africa, right now?—Jean-Luc ardently:—Look Flora, I couldn't tell you before to scare you off. But the whole truth is: I Love you with all my heart . . . !—She prevents him from talking:—Look, I don't know?—Jean-Luc eagerly:—Please let me speak? I've felt in love with you, from the moment, when you boldly stood up against Pirates!—He stops; takes a deep breathe; then is telling more. Jean-Luc ardently:—And in Hospital, when I did that surgery on you! You're my idol and I admire you . . .—,He stops; taken breaths; Jean-Luc looks with plead, as be sadden:—My greatest fear is that, if you leave now, I may never see you again, Fleur?—Flora seems is confused:— Jean-Luc, I value your feelings for me. But chain of the event that I've got through, avoid me to think of any relationships, now! I'm sorry, Jean-Luc that I hurt your feelings but . . .—, He's ardently:—I know, Flora that your health, even so being improved? Still you were traumatized, and need to get well over time! I'm ready to wait on your decision, as long as you need! I love you, Fleur, remember that!

Long after Jean-Luc left, she reflects to herself; so far definite on:—If facing real danger . . ."—She begins crying . . . She stops; takes a deep breathe; be convinced; then has alleged:—From be usurped—to overcome obstacles, which fate toss in. Like usurper resists to be at victory! In my triumph to a most crucial sensation for one—staying alive and to be free!—Up till now she has lesser kept in mind her ex-; and lastly reconciled of her failed marriage. So she is given her word:— . . . forget my husband! While he had faked been in love, in fact he never was! Nor the least, cause Mbeki threw me conquer violence!—

Before leaving for the airport in a bid to fly back to her native-home Flora is said good-byes; and flying away . . .

CHAPTER 26

A fair six months have gone by. African night; in a miniature Tavern at the table is seeing Jean-Luc, who's sitting at wooden table parallel to counter, sipping whisky from a glass—scrutiny he is deep into thoughts. On other side over counter is visible a man of an African appear, bartender Makah—is meticulously checks Jean-Luc out. The bartender is standing parallel from Jean-Luc, on the other side of a counter; and personally being serving all those customers; with Jean-Luc counted; he is deep into he's thoughts; on other side sees a man bartender is often distracting Jean-Luc; in a way of asking aloud; seen he is concerned:—What can I get you sir?—Has asked an African man, the bar owner that worked here as a bartender—Makah. Jean-Luc firmly; loudly reacting:—Another shot of whisky, please!—Looking into an empty glass, Jean-Luc is replying, loudly, and points to a glass:—Splash me more, whisky!—Jean-Luc puts a hand into his pocket; and is reaching for Cigarettes; he then lights up one. Next he deeply inhales cigarette smoke. As he looks toward entrance, where out of blue with bluish smoke—has developed aerial by itself into cigarette-rings of Flora's silhouette. Flora beams at him; and he seems being into hallucinations; as far as this image remained for a few minutes. Until . . .

A strange voice brings Jean-Luc back to the reality.

All through analysis of Doctor's condition; Makah is solemn but firmly says-so for:—Doc! I think you've got more than enough drinking? Why don't you sip coffee, instead? I bet it'll put you back on your feet, Doc!—Jean-Luc in his turn tells the bartender of his emotions, anxiously:—I'm having such a deep love for Flora. But she hasn't even realized of my passion and feelings for her. Flora once has told me, she doesn't want to be usurped again . . .—He is breathing deep, and has prolonged:—Well, now I'm the usurped! What am I to do now? I'm miserable. I want to drink, and forget about the whole thing!—Instead a bartender is suggested that Jean-Luc does:—You know, Doc why won't you express your feelings to Flora input with writing her a letter? Do it the old fashion way! And don't give up on you're Love, Doc!—Is indicating

Makah. As Jean-Luc is raised a glass:—I hope for a future with Flora . . .—

Later that night in his place Jean-Luc sits at a computer— writes E-mail to Flora:—Dear, Flora! I hope you didn't forget me . . . ?—

CHAPTER 27

Next step Jean-Luc grasps; is seen his arrival at Flora's home, in New Haven, Connecticut—faraway at the side of a porch, where Whitmore's residence is located, where has emerged Jean-Luc Cartier. He buzzes three times. Flora appears on the porch, and is looking amazed to see him in her hometown. She looks at a complete loss now. Flora's lifts a hand up and placed on her chest:—Jean-Luc! It's really you? Stop. She seems is avid; and gazed at him, as says-so:—What are you doing here? How . . . ? Did you come to see me?—Jean-Luc looks into her eyes; talks calmly:—Of course! I couldn't wait any longer. I was long to see you . . .—, She stops him; her eyes glowing:—I thought of you too, Jean-Luc. Why won't you come in? I would like you to meet my family?—He shakes awkwardly with his limbs, and is shy:—Are you sure about this, Fleur?—She beams and ducks her head:—I'm sure. Please, come in Jean-Luc!—She steps aside that invites Jean-Luc into her family home.

Those two spend heaps of time in each other's company are walking on the New Haven's streets . . .

So, Flora has become very much attached to Jean-Luc . . .

Soon Flora and Jean-Luc are seeing on track of dating.

It's typical Saturday afternoon on the New Haven Streets. The Sun is bright; it's late autumn; cloudy. In a heart of the city appears Flora is walking alongside Jean-Luc. Next the pair stops; and began kissing; where that public is strolling in area with a peculiar look at those two. Flora and Jean-Luc are in flavor of showing their true feelings to each-other—inept having been in love . . .

In entry hall becomes visible Flora and Jean-Luc is just having entered a reception area in a disco club. After paying for the tickets this pair is strolling straight into a dancing hall.

Later that evening—the pair has created on their own of self-reliance for duration of a dancing session; they're watching other pairs dancing. Next they are using vivid lights for passionate kissing, and whispering amid that period. Flora in enchant whisper:—I feel superb! My only wish is for the tick slowly to set on,—Jean-Luc beams:—Bar, it's good to know that your feelings are convinced. So am I, Fleur. Flora is breathing in; hearing her tone changed of regret and she tells:—Will, you be okay, going to the Hostel alone? If I won't be home on time, I'm afraid my parents might get ballistic . . .—stop, she then tempts:—Jean-Luck I invite you to spend the night in my house? Do you except . . . ?—

Next sees Flora and Jean-Luc are tow—into courting . . .

Lastly Jean-Luc has guts—proposed of marriage to Flora.

He is keenly:—Fleur, I do love you! And I'm asking you to marry me! What do say?—Her face turns pink:—Jean-Luc, for those time, I've become attached to you! My emotions . . .—Flora stop takes breaths; looks in his eyes; cheeks pink, says ardently:—I have fallen in love with you, Jean-Luc. And my answer is—yes!-

At Flora and Jean-Luc wedding are heard words of wisdom:—True love can be found even in the darkest and through toughest times in one's life; since it's really exist!—

CHAPTER 28

A view Flora lands on the surface ground in Africa, where all her troubles had begun all but two years ago. Now Flora returns back here—is walking around airport spots. She is dressed in nicely suits her. Her wisdom that:—When I left Tanzania almost two years ago . . . I had thought deep in my heart, one way or another, I have to returned back to Africa!-

Meantime Flora bows her head down; takes gulps of air—accepting wisdom of life, and continual:—Our heart-to-heart with Jean-Luc has made me backing that human must act with compassion towards one another. I arrived here alone, as being free of violence. I am woman I want to start anew life with a man that I truly love; and be loved by!-

Back to reality: Still holds flowers that Jean-Luc gave her; Flora sits on the beach, barefoot, her shoes by; concomitantly be lost in thoughts—her reminiscences of the whole thing, which she had endured in order to get, where she is right now.

From nowhere, a soft, familiar accent with warmth slowly beckons Flora towards reality—saying her name over and over. This is Jean-Luc that goes down on his knees. Sees Flora's eyes are glowing; as she hugs Jean-Luc. He does embrace her likewise; and both are holding close in each other's arms. Jean-Luc is loud, but fretful:—Flora, are you alright?—Her responds:—Thanks, God, I am now! You know, Jean-Luc I is waiting for true Love like that, in years to come?—She indicates. He is with a wide smile:—I will love you forever!—Flora inhales a gulp of air:—I love you too, and will do evermore!-

Flora and Jean-Luc are getting up; footing on; lean into each other with a spark of attraction—are forgetting those around them. Follows they're both having embraced into passionate kissing . . .

Captured sight they're not alone in the site, given that public freezes, is watching the pair with jealousy. Out of love Jean-Luc and Flora are pouring into kissing.

Next Flora and Jean-Luc Cartier are walking hand-in-hand towards the sunset; and vanishing in the horizon.

THE END.